MURDER AT THE CHURCH

A Cottonwood Springs Cozy Mystery - Book 2

BY

DIANNE HARMAN

Published by: Dianne Harman
www.dianneharman.com

Interior, cover design and website by
Vivek Rajan

ISBN: 9781729173930

CONTENTS

Acknowledgments

1 Prologue   1

2 Chapter One   9

3 Chapter Two   17

4 Chapter Three   26

5 Chapter Four   33

6 Chapter Five   39

7 Chapter Six   44

8 Chapter Seven   51

9 Chapter Eight   59

10 Chapter Nine   64

11 Chapter Ten   73

12 Chapter Eleven   78

13 Chapter Twelve   86

14 Chapter Thirteen   93

15 Chapter Fourteen   101

16 Chapter Fifteen   109

17 Chapter Sixteen   118

18 Chapter Seventeen   126

19 Chapter Eighteen   135

20	Epilogue	144
21	Recipes	149
22	About Dianne	156
23	Coming Soon!	158

ACKNOWLEDGMENTS

Thanks to all of you who bought the first book in this new series, Murder in Cottonwood Springs, and made it a bestseller. Many of you wrote asking when the next one would be published. Well, here it is!

Committing murder in a church is about the most sacrilegious act a person can do. However, sometimes events just have to happen in a certain way, or so the Muse that comes to me at night when I'm sleeping tells me!

There are several people I want to thank for their help in getting this book published. Krystal, Meghan, Connie, Vivek, and of course, my in-house editor, Tom. I know the readers appreciate all the work you do, so they can continue to read about Brigid's adventures in the small mountainous town of Cottonwood Springs, Colorado.

I hope you enjoy this book and yes, a third one is being written and will be available in the near future! Thanks again for your support.

Win FREE Paperbacks every week!

Go to www.dianneharman.com/freepaperback.html and get your FREE copies of Dianne's books and favorite recipes immediately by signing up for her newsletter.

Once you've signed up for her newsletter you're eligible to win three paperbacks. One lucky winner is picked every week. Hurry before the offer ends!

PROLOGUE

Maggie Lewis was totally frustrated. She chewed on what was left of her bitten-down fingernails, willing the strength to resist temptation. She knew she had to stay sober, if not for herself, then for Holly. She'd already put her teenage daughter through too much trauma in her young life, such as men coming in and out of the house at all hours of day and night and seeing her mother either drunk or high on drugs most of the time.

She knew she'd been a terrible mother for the first twelve years of Holly's life, but now that Mike Loomis, her main drug supplier, was in prison, it was the perfect time for her to get clean. What she hadn't counted on was just how difficult it was going to be.

Maggie had reached out for help, because she knew she couldn't do it on her own. Missy, Father Jerome's wife, had been a huge help by giving her the names of different resources she could call upon. It had been weeks since she'd last had a drink or used drugs, although neither had been far from her thoughts the whole time. The depression that came with getting clean was still hard for her, but she was coping, and seeing the hope in Holly's eyes was enough to keep her away from booze and drugs. For the first time since she'd given birth to Holly, Maggie had made her daughter her top priority. She was ashamed to admit that putting herself first all those years had been a lot easier.

She stood up from the couch and walked into the tiny kitchen of the two-bedroom trailer where the two of them lived. It was just after midnight, but she was used to staying up late, usually until three in the morning. She worked nights at the local candy factory, so for her, it really wasn't all that late.

Maggie opened a kitchen cabinet, took out a cup of noodles, and started to boil some water. It was nice being able to use the stove again. The money she saved from not spending whatever she had on her addictions had allowed her to work out a payment plan with the utility company.

Even though she knew it wasn't that big of a deal to most people, to be able to do it had meant a lot to her. Maggie had grown up in Cottonwood Springs, and when she'd gone to the utility company to see what she could work out, she found out she and the manager had been in the same class in high school. She told him how hard she was trying and asked if he could help her. It had hurt what was left of her pride to admit how much she was struggling financially, and she had said a silent prayer of thanks when he'd said yes.

It was good to know that people were rooting for her and willing to help. She couldn't remember the last time the different utilities in the trailer had all been on at the same time. What lingered in her memory were the times she'd showered in cold water, because she couldn't pay the gas bill.

As she was waiting for the water to start boiling, her cell phone buzzed, pulling her out of her thoughts. She grabbed her old flip phone and opened it. It was just as she thought, another text from Billy. She sighed.

Hey baby, why won't you answer me?

Maggie tossed the phone down on the kitchen counter, not even bothering to reply. She'd told Billy more than once that she wasn't interested in being with him anymore, but he didn't seem to get the point. He refused to listen to her, still lost in the depths of his own addiction and demons. Maggie knew if she was going to stay sober, there was no place in her life for Billy. She'd made her decision, and there was no turning back from it. Not this time.

She poured the boiling water into the cup and waited for the noodles to soften. She'd begged Billy to get clean with her, but he'd just laughed. Instead, he'd started driving into Denver to find his fix, and now he was selling to the addicts who had relied on Mike for their supply. Her phone buzzed again.

Come on, I know you're awake.

She stirred the noodles as she leaned back against the counter. Taking a deep breath, she counted to ten. Fighting the depression and anxiety during the past few weeks had really taken its toll on her. As she ate, she listened to the old familiar excuses boiling up in her mind. *It's just one drink,* they said. *One hit won't hurt anything.*

She'd learned from the meetings at the church that what she heard was her addiction talking. Her insecurities and doubts were voicing their complaints, trying to bring her down. Trying to separate those voices from her own was tough. The addiction didn't want to let go of her, no matter how much she wanted to let go of it. *Hmmm, a bit like Billy,* she thought.

Maggie began to pace the length of the small trailer, which didn't take more than a handful of steps. She looked at herself in the full-length mirror mounted on the back of the bedroom door. Her mousy brown hair was pulled up in a messy bun, but thankfully she was starting to get some color back in her face. She'd gained some weight, so the only thing that fit her these days were loose tee shirts and sweats.

Maggie knew she was going to have to spend money on a couple of pairs of jeans pretty soon. That wasn't necessarily a bad thing, but she needed to buy a few clothes for Holly first. She was planning on taking her next paycheck and spending it all on her daughter. Holly deserved it after what she'd been through.

Maggie heard her phone buzz on the kitchen counter again. She didn't even bother to look at it, knowing who it would be. Billy was the only one who messaged her this late at night.

She stepped into her small bedroom, looking for her jacket. The spring air was pleasant but cool. Maggie thought a walk might distract her and help her get rid of some of the anxiety tightening her chest, at least for a little while, and then she'd be able to get some sleep. She wanted to get up early, so she could spend some time with Holly.

She grabbed a notepad from the kitchen counter and wrote a quick note to Holly in case she woke up in the middle of the night and noticed that Maggie was gone. Maggie knew her daughter would automatically assume she'd left to go find a fix. It hurt to even think that, but she knew it was the truth. How many times in Holly's life had a nightmare woken her up and then she'd found out mommy wasn't there? More times than she could count.

"Went out for a walk to clear my mind," she wrote. "I'll only be gone a few minutes. Love you to the moon and back, Mom."

As she opened the door and quietly shut it behind her, Maggie thought about everything she'd put her daughter through. Holly had acted like an adult from the time she was a small child, because she'd had no choice. Maggie had only stayed sober long enough to work and get a paycheck. As soon as she was finished with work, she was gone, getting high and drunk.

Holly paid the bills, bought groceries, and cooked the meals. There were even a few nights when Holly had taken care of her mother. She'd never complained or spoken out against Maggie, just quietly cleaning her up after her sick binges, withdrawing into herself a little more each time it happened. Tears trailed down Maggie's cheeks as she walked through the dark trailer park, thinking of the past.

She knew she needed to go to the one place that always calmed her and made her feel at peace with the world. She was so intent on her thoughts she didn't notice that someone was following her. They kept their distance, far enough behind her that their footsteps couldn't be heard on the pavement. They weren't sure where she was going, only that they were going to follow her, and they didn't want her to know they were only a short distance behind her.

Maggie looked up at the clouds sliding across the moon. With the crisp air filling her lungs, she was starting to feel a bit better. Things had been so tough lately. She'd anticipated the physical symptoms of withdrawal. Those weren't all that tough to manage, after all, she'd been through worse.

No, it was the mental aspect she hadn't been prepared for. Add to that the fact that Billy had been harassing her ever since she'd broken off their relationship, and she was struggling to cope. Even though she hadn't answered him for days, actually weeks, he still continued to text her. Maybe a bit of distance would help him clear his mind and see what he was doing to himself.

As the large white church came into view, Maggie felt the tension in her shoulders relax. It was funny how the church had that effect on her now. Before, when she'd driven by the church she'd made jokes that she couldn't ever set foot in the old building, because she'd burst into flames. Now it was her refuge from all the terrible things she'd done, a place where she found comfort, peace and unconditional forgiveness, even though she couldn't yet forgive herself.

The old white church looked like something out of a painting. A tall steeple tower rose from the sloped roof and was backdropped against the nearby trees. The rectory, where the priest's family lived, was behind it. Jordan Blair was the priest of the Episcopal church and his wife was Missy. Maggie had come to think of both of them as saints in disguise, because they'd helped so many people in the small town, including her.

As she climbed the stone steps leading up to the large red wooden doors of the church, a sense of peace enveloped Maggie. Here she felt safe from the outside world. Within the church's walls she'd found her own religion. Although she didn't completely agree with everything that was said in the church, she felt like it was helping her make her way to a better of life. She knew she had a lot of atoning to do for all the sins she'd committed, but she was confident that God knew how hard she was working to make a better life for Holly and her.

She quietly walked up the center aisle of the church, not wanting to disturb anyone who might also be present at this late hour. She looked around the pews wondering if anyone else was there seeking an audience with God, but for the moment, she had the church all to herself. The beautiful stained-glass windows were dark at this time of night, but that didn't keep her from admiring them.

She was fascinated by the way they were made with simple pieces of colored glass, cut, and then pieced together to create beautiful images. Maggie liked to think that each piece was kind of like a person. They may not be perfect on their own, but once a group of them came together, something magical could happen. The deep red curtains along the side walls of the church were pulled back and tied with golden ropes with tassels making everything seem regal and elegant.

Maggie continued to the front of the church and knelt down on the prayer bench below the large cross on the front wall of the church. She folded her hands and bowed her head and began praying. "Hey, God, it's me again," she started. "I'm really struggling tonight. I need some strength. I've failed terribly as a mother, and I know Holly deserves a better life. She's seen more than any child should, and I'm scared."

She paused, feeling a lump begin to form in her throat. "I don't want her to grow up and be like me. Please save her from that, no matter what it takes. I want her to have a better life. She deserves it. She's so smart, and she has so much potential."

The person who had been following Maggie quietly slipped in the front door of the church. They paused to make sure Maggie hadn't heard them enter. When she didn't turn to look in their direction, they crept up the side aisle of the church, the shadows and the curtains hiding their presence, their footsteps muffled by the thick carpet.

As Maggie continued to pray, she raised her voice slightly. "I'm still working through trying to forgive myself for everything I've done—the stealing, the lying, and the cheating. I regret so many things. Please help me. Father Jordan and Missy have been amazing, but I haven't told them everything. I'm afraid to. I'm sure they know some of it, because Cottonwood Springs isn't that big of a town. I'm not proud of what I've done in the past, and no one knows better than me that some of it is really bad."

The person paused next to the first row of pews. Maggie was still far enough away she wouldn't be able to see them unless she turned around. They listened to what she was saying.

"I know I've hurt so many people, like Mark, MaryAnn, Frank, George, Billy, even Sam, not to mention all the others. There's just so much wrong that I've done, but please, more than anything, I beg you to help me stay away from Billy. I know he'll pull me back down if I see him or talk to him. Please help me. I'm desperate."

Listening to Maggie talk about all those people enraged the person who had been following her. When they heard their name recited by Maggie, everything came bubbling to the surface. Pure rage filled their chest as they removed one of the golden ropes that was holding back a portion of the curtain. Creeping up behind Maggie, in a flash they had the rope wrapped tightly around her neck.

It took Maggie a moment to realize what was happening. As the rope tightened, she raised her arm and tried to push it away, gasping for breath. When she realized she couldn't get it loose, her hands clawed at the person who was behind her. Her fingernails dug into their arm, scratching the bare skin. No matter what she did, the rope was held tightly against her neck, burning her skin.

As she struggled to get her breath, things began to get fuzzy and dark around the edges. She looked up at the figure of Jesus looking down on her from the cross. Her last conscious thought was how sympathetic his eyes were. Her killer continued to pull the rope tightly around her neck until her body no longer moved.

They removed the rope from her throat and wrapped it around their hand, knowing how dangerous it would be to leave it, since they weren't wearing gloves. It wasn't as if the strangulation was planned, it just happened. They looked around, but no one had come into the church, and they quietly crept out of the church. It was late, and if they hurried home, no one would know that they were responsible for the murder of Maggie Lewis.

CHAPTER ONE

Brigid had just walked through the front door and was headed for the kitchen for a glass of water when her cell phone rang. She looked at the caller ID and saw that it was her friend Missy.

"Hi, Missy," she said.

"Good morning, Brigid. Are you busy or can you talk for a minute?" she asked.

"I was just getting a glass of water, so obviously I'm not all that busy. What can I do for you?" Brigid continued walking towards the kitchen and took a glass from the cabinet. Jett, her large black Newfoundland dog, was eagerly drinking from his water dish. They'd just returned from their morning jog and both of them were thirsty.

"I have a favor to ask. We host the local Alcoholics Anonymous meetings at the church, and I usually have plenty of help, but none of them can do it this evening. I was wondering if you'd be willing to give me a hand?"

"When is it?" Brigid asked. She was usually free, but she didn't want to commit to something and then have to cancel. She leaned her hip against the counter, taking a drink from her glass.

"The meeting's tonight at 7:00."

"Sure, that's not a problem. I'd be glad to assist, although I've never been to one of their meetings, so I don't know what to expect," Brigid said, glad she could help Missy.

"Oh, thanks, Brigid. It really means a lot to me, and the fact you've never attended a meeting is fine. I'd never attended one either before we started doing them here at the church, but I suppose that's a good thing," Missy said. "I have one more favor to ask. Could you bring some type of a snack? I like to have something available for the people attending the meetings. Normally I take care of it, but I'm swamped today."

"I'd be happy to," Brigid said. She opened her cabinets to look for ingredients. "I think I have the stuff to make some cream cheese brownies. People always seem to like those. Would that do?"

"That would be perfect," Missy said brightly. "Thanks again. I'd love to talk, but I really do have a number of things I need to do."

"I understand. See you tonight," Brigid said as she ended the call.

She was on her way to the bathroom to take a shower when she heard a knock on the front door. Brigid looked through the small window and saw Linc on the other side, smiling at her. She laughed and opened the door.

"I was just getting ready to hop in the shower. If you want to wait a couple of minutes, you can hang out with Jett. He'd love it." As soon as his name was mentioned, the big dog ran to the door and bumped against her leg. Linc walked in, and she shut the door behind him.

"Take your time. Jett and I haven't had any guy time for a while." He'd already started playing with Jett, who was jumping around and obviously eager to play with Linc.

"Enjoy the guy time. I'll be back in a few minutes."

She headed down the hall, and as she walked by the guest

bedroom, she glanced into it. She'd tried rearranging the room and shutting the door, but it hadn't helped. In her mind's eye, she could still see Rachele's laptop sitting on the desk, the story of her best friend Lucy's murder displayed on the screen. Even the thought of it made her shiver.

Brigid shook her head, took a deep breath, and a few moments later she opened her closet and began picking out clothes to wear. Grabbing a pair of jeans and a white cotton shirt, she headed into the bathroom and turned on the shower. It didn't take long before the warm water soothed her body, which was already feeling a bit stiff from the run.

She'd started working on getting in shape a few weeks earlier and was beginning to feel pleased with the results. With everything that had happened when she was investigating Lucy's death, Brigid felt as though she needed to be able to protect herself, and having a strong body was part of the process.

Linc had been visiting her quite often lately, but neither one of them had made a commitment. For now, they simply enjoyed being with one another. After having been in a bad marriage, Brigid was enjoying her independence, and he was fine with that. Neither one of them wanted to put a label on what they had, afraid it might ruin it, so they'd decided to let things just unfold naturally, however that may be.

When she was out of the shower and dressed, she joined Linc and Jett in the great room. She couldn't help but laugh. Jett had Linc on the ground, licking his face. Linc was trying to avoid the slobbery licks, but without much success.

"Hate to tell you this, but whatever game you're playing, I think Jett won," she said. Jett hopped off of Linc and rushed over to greet Brigid, tail wagging, as if she'd just come home from an extended trip, rather than walking down the hall returning from her shower.

"Yeah, I'd have to agree with you," Linc said as he got up off the floor. "How was the run?"

"It's not number one on my list of fun things to do, but it seems to be working, and I think it's great exercise for Jett. As big as he is, he needs some." She turned and looked at the dog who had left her side and climbed up on the old loveseat in the corner that had become his bed. He was already snoring softly.

"That's good," Linc said. He paused and clapped his hands, "Drum roll, please. I have some news." Linc looked nervous. He knew how Brigid felt about their relationship, and he felt like there was a big grey area about what their future looked like.

"Oh, and I assume you're going to share it," she said, sitting down in her favorite armchair.

Linc screwed up his face, as if he was trying hard to think about exactly how he wanted to phrase it. "It's like this, Brigid, my parents are coming for a visit." He quickly put his hand up. "You don't have to meet them if you don't want to. It's completely up to you. They're going to be staying overnight at my house, kind of a landing place because my mother has been wanting to come see my home..." he said, letting his sentence trail off.

"That's great!" Brigid said. "Aren't you happy about it?" She sensed his anxiety, but she wasn't quite sure what was worrying him.

"Of course, I am, but if you don't feel our relationship is at a place where you want to meet them yet, I'd completely understand. In which case, we will have to postpone our dinner tomorrow night, because I just found out they were coming." Linc sat down nervously on the couch. He was hoping Brigid would want to meet them. His first wife and his parents hadn't gotten along well at all. He didn't know where things were going with Brigid and him, but he knew he'd feel a lot better about it if both sides could at least tolerate each other.

Brigid thought about it for a moment before answering. "I'd very much like to meet them if you want me to, Linc. The opportunity is presenting itself, so we may as well take advantage of it."

Linc visibly relaxed. "Great," he said. "I have some work I have to do today, but if you aren't busy tonight maybe we could watch a movie or something."

"I'm sorry, Linc, but I can't tonight," she said. "I told Missy I'd help her out at the church."

"Okay. Just thought I'd ask. I'll call you with the details," he said as he stood up. Brigid stood as well and gave him a hug.

"Have a good day," she said before they kissed goodbye. Jett opened one eye and sleepily looked at them, deciding it was more important for him to stay where he was than accompany Linc to the door.

"You, too," he said.

*****

That evening when Brigid pulled into the church parking lot, she parked as close to the back door as possible. Clouds had moved in. The weather report had said there was a chance it would rain, and it looked like they were finally right. Brigid picked up the tray of brownies she'd made and hurried into the church.

"It's starting to get stormy out there," she said after greeting Missy.

"Oh, really? I've been inside for a couple of hours, so I hadn't noticed. I hope everyone makes it here okay," she said with a worried expression on her face.

"Why wouldn't they?" Brigid asked as she set the brownies down on the table.

"A couple of them live here in town and walk to the meetings. They don't own a car," Missy said simply.

Brigid was surprised, not that people had to walk to the meeting, but that she'd taken something as simple as her car for granted. She had a feeling she was going to learn some other things tonight that she'd also taken for granted.

Brigid and Missy began setting up the chairs and getting things ready for the meeting. Before long, people started arriving. Brigid did her best to put a name with a face, but she knew there was no way she was going to be able to remember all of them. Eventually, a woman walked through the door and Brigid noticed Missy heaving a sigh of relief.

"I'm so glad you made it," Missy said as she hurried over to the woman. The woman had short chestnut-brown hair with freckles dotting the bridge of her nose. She was thin and wore a jacket that was far too big for her slender frame.

"It started to sprinkle just as I got here," she said smiling. "I took that as a good omen."

"Maggie, this is my good friend Brigid. She's helping me out tonight," Missy said, introducing them.

"Nice to meet you," Maggie said shaking Brigid's hand.

"Nice to meet you, too," Brigid said.

"Maggie's been coming to our meetings for a few weeks now, and she's doing great, especially considering her circumstances. I'm really proud of her," Missy said as she warmly put her hand on Maggie's shoulder.

The woman blushed and looked away. "I'm not special, Missy. Plenty of people stay sober every day," she said dismissing the praise.

"It's a great accomplishment," Brigid said with a smile. "You should be proud of yourself."

Maggie looked at Brigid, surprised by what she'd said, and then allowed herself a real smile. "Thank you."

A rumble of thunder shook the floor just as Missy began to raise her voice. "Alright everyone. Grab a soft drink or coffee and a snack if you'd like and take a seat. We'll get started when everyone's gotten settled."

Brigid took a seat along one side of the room and silenced her phone. She sat back and listened to each person stand up and speak about their struggles to stay sober. She heard the backstory given by those who stood and along with others, applauded their successes. As the meeting wore on she found herself secretly rooting for each one of them. She'd never felt so close to a group of strangers in her entire life. She couldn't even begin to imagine what it must have taken for each of them to go to their first meeting.

When it was over, everyone continued to talk as they headed toward the exit, except for Maggie, who remained seated. "Would you like another brownie, Maggie?" Missy asked as she walked over to the snack table and picked one up.

"Yes, please. They were wonderful." She stood up from where she was sitting and joined Missy.

Missy looked up at Brigid and said, "You don't have to stay. After the Alcoholics Anonymous meeting we have a Narcotics Anonymous meeting."

"Well, don't you still need help?" Brigid asked. "I'm happy to stick around for a while longer."

"No, but thanks. Maggie is the only one who attends. It's not really an official NA meeting, but we do our best," Missy said as she smiled at Maggie.

"Apparently, I'm the only one who wants to get clean around here," Maggie said with a laugh.

"I'd like to stay, if you don't mind. Maybe there's something I can do," Brigid said.

Maggie smiled thinly. "That's up to you, but you may not like me very much after you hear about the things I've done."

CHAPTER TWO

"Your past doesn't need to define your future, Maggie," Missy told the younger woman. "Everyone's made mistakes. It's what we do after we acknowledge them that shows who we really are."

"Intellectually I know that, but emotionally I'm still struggling to cope with what I did when I wasn't in my right mind. At the time, it seemed like the right thing to do. Now that I'm sober, I see how twisted my thinking was. I'm left with what I've done, and believe me, those aren't very happy memories." Maggie's head hung down. A moment later she turned to Brigid and smiled. "I promise I'm not always this sad. It's just been a rough week for me."

"Don't worry about it," Brigid said. "You'll probably feel better if you get everything off your chest."

Maggie nodded and turned back to Missy. "I know I'm supposed to take things one day at a time, but there's one person who's really making that difficult for me."

"Let me guess. Billy. But you expected that, didn't you?" Missy asked gently, although her words were forceful. She was being kind with Maggie, but she also knew there were times when you had to show a bit of sternness to someone in Maggie's position. "You need to let him go, Maggie. He's a thorn in your side, and if you don't let him go, he'll undo all the good you've done. He can't do anything but bring you trouble."

"I know," Maggie said. "I try to avoid him, because I don't want to talk to him, but occasionally I've had to. Missy, you know how hard it can be in this small town to avoid people. I don't answer his texts or phone calls, and if I'm in a position where I have to talk to him, I keep it short and sweet." Maggie twisted her hands in her lap. "It's all so hard. Giving up the drugs is easy compared to the booze. Everywhere you look, you see it, even on television and at the movies."

Brigid couldn't imagine what it was like to completely give up something so readily available. Then she remembered how she'd been struggling with giving up sweets while trying get in shape and how she'd rationalized having a candy bar the other day while she was grocery shopping. It had been a spur of the moment purchase, caused simply by seeing it. Maybe they were different substances, but she had a sense of just how tough the struggle must be for Maggie. Willpower was often in short supply just when one needed it most.

"I admire you," Brigid said. "You're lucky to have Missy and her support. Just keep doing what you're doing and surely Billy will get the hint. Some people are just a bit more stubborn. Sounds like he's one of them. Have you tried getting him to come to the meetings with you?"

Maggie nodded. "I wanted him to get sober with me, but he laughed and said he'd never step foot in a church. He thinks all they do is brainwash people. He's an atheist." She shrugged. "Billy took over selling meth when Mike Loomis got locked up. He won't give up dealing drugs, because he says the money is so much easier than getting a real job."

"Forget Billy. I think you're doing great," Missy said, leaning forward and rubbing Maggie's arm. "You know I'm here most of the time. In fact, sometimes when I can't sleep at night, I go in the chapel and say a silent prayer. Think about it. It might help you when you feel anxious."

Missy looked at her watch and sighed. "I have to make a few phone calls. Don't worry about cleaning up. I'll get it later. Have a good rest of the evening, Brigid, and thank you again for helping." She waved as she hurried through the wooden door that led upstairs to the church office.

Brigid stood up and began putting away the chairs. She smiled when she saw Maggie doing the same. They both worked quietly for a few moments and then Brigid said, "It sounds like you're doing really well, and I'm happy for you."

"Thanks, but it's something I have to do for my daughter. If it wasn't for Holly, I think I'd have given up long ago." Maggie stacked the last chair on the cart and pushed it against the wall.

"I didn't know you had a daughter. How old is she?" Brigid asked as she wrapped up the brownies and cleaned off the table.

"Thirteen. She's great and really smart. I don't know where she gets it from," Maggie said, laughing. "She goes to the library every day during school summer vacation to study the subjects she's going to have the following year, so she'll have a leg up on everyone."

"Wow! That's impressive. I bet her teachers love her," Brigid said with a smile.

"I don't know. I've never been to a Parent Teacher conference," Maggie said softly, looking down at the floor.

Brigid paused, realizing she'd accidentally struck a nerve. "I'm sure the teachers aren't worried about her. Anyway, from what I hear, those things are more for the kids who are struggling, and it sure doesn't sound like she is." Once everything was put away, Brigid and Maggie headed towards the door. "That's probably something you could look forward to doing in the future. I'll bet your daughter would be thrilled."

Maggie visibly brightened and smiled. "Thanks. I hadn't thought of that. I've often thought Holly doesn't want me there, like she's ashamed of me. If so, I wouldn't blame her. I hope that's not always going to be the case." She pushed the door open and stepped out into the covered area beside the church. They hadn't heard the rain when they'd been inside the church, but once they were outside, they realized rain was pouring down.

Brigid noticed Maggie's look of apprehension as she stared at the rain. "Why don't you let me give you a ride home?"

"That's okay, you don't have to," Maggie said, "I'm sure it's out of your way."

"No, I absolutely insist. Come on," Brigid jogged over to her car and quickly climbed in. After a moment of hesitation, Maggie joined her.

"I really appreciate this," Maggie said as she shut the door. "Normally walking isn't a big deal, but when it rains like this…" She pulled her thin coat tighter around her.

"Don't even think about it," Brigid said. She looked down at the brownies in her hands. After Maggie had buckled her seatbelt she handed them to Maggie. "Here, why don't you take these home to your daughter so you two can share them?"

Maggie's face lit up. "She'd love that. Thanks. That's one of the nicest things anyone has ever done for me." She gave Brigid the directions to get to her home and leaned back in her seat. "Have you ever done anything you really regretted?" Maggie finally asked.

Brigid thought for a moment. "Of course. I think that's something that comes with being human. We all do things we're ashamed of later." She looked sideways at Maggie and saw that she was looking out the window, lost in her thoughts. "I think it's what you do to set things right that really determine who you are as a person. Even if you can't fix it, if you just work hard at not being that person anymore, or making the same mistake, that's what counts."

"I've hurt a lot of people, Brigid. I've been a thief, a homewrecker, and a lousy mother. I don't know if I could ever make it up to all of them," Maggie said with a sigh.

Brigid turned down the street that led to the trailer park. The rain was finally starting to let up and there was a sliver of moonlight peeking through the clouds.

"It's the third one on the left with the yellow siding," Maggie said as Brigid drove slowly between the trailers. "Why don't you come in and have a brownie with us?" Maggie asked. "You could meet my daughter, Holly."

"I'd love that," Brigid said, as she stopped her car in front of Maggie's trailer. Although she didn't particularly think it was safe to go into the home of a random stranger, in this case she felt it would be rude not to. Besides, she was really enjoying getting to know Maggie, and thought Maggie could probably use a few sober friends to help her on her way.

"I apologize for the way the place looks. I know it isn't very attractive. I haven't exactly had my priorities straight." Brigid could tell Maggie was embarrassed by the broken porch boards and the loose siding on the trailer.

"Don't even think about it for a minute," Brigid said. "You have more important things on your mind right now."

Maggie turned and smiled at Brigid as she opened the front door. "Holly, we have company," Maggie said in a loud voice as she entered the small trailer. Brigid looked around, taking everything in. It wasn't big, but it was clean. The countertops in the nearby kitchen were worn with use and the old floral couch was sagging and covered with quilts. The grey carpet was threadbare, but all of that was superficial. She could tell by how clean the trailer was that it was well taken care of.

A pretty young blonde girl came down the narrow hall and smiled politely. Her sweet round face had freckles like her mother, but her eyes were large and blue. She was wearing a pair of cut-off jean shorts and a faded rock band shirt.

"Holly, this is Brigid Barnes. She's one of Missy's friends. She gave me a ride home and offered us the rest of the brownies she'd made. I invited her in to have one of them with us."

Holly's eyes lit up when she saw the brownies, and Brigid couldn't help but smile. There was something about having others enjoy the food she made that always pleased her.

"Thanks. Those looks amazing," Holly said. "Want me to get some plates, Mom?"

"Would you please?" she answered as she set the brownies down on the counter. "I'm afraid we only have water and milk to drink," Maggie said apologetically.

"I'd love a glass of milk. Thank you," Brigid said. She watched as mother and daughter served up three brownies and three glasses of milk. Maggie handed Brigid hers and gestured towards the front room area.

"Let's go in there. We can sit and talk for a minute," Maggie said.

"Holly, I hear from your mom that you're a pretty smart young lady," Brigid said to start the conversation.

"I mean, I guess so," Holly said bashfully. "I get some of the highest grades in my class."

"That's something to be proud of," said Brigid. "I struggled in science and math. They were not my favorite subjects, not by a long shot."

They continued to talk about Cottonwood Springs, their favorite desserts, and life as a teenager. Brigid found herself growing fond of the two. There was an inner strength in Holly that must have come from having to take care of herself for so long. On one hand, Brigid felt sorry for the girl for not getting to be a kid while she could, yet on the other hand, she saw how her mother's illness was the very thing that had led to Holly getting good grades. Rather than making excuses, Holly had learned to just work harder and take responsibility for herself.

At one point, Holly felt comfortable enough to say, "It doesn't help living in a trailer park and wearing everyone's old clothes that they donated to the church. Some girls have seen me at the library when I'm there using the internet, and I know they're talking about me behind my back."

"Don't worry about those other girls at school," Brigid told her. "I think each of us had some girl that was the bane of our existence when we were growing up. Ignore them. Just do what you need to do and try not to let any of them get to you."

Brigid sensed that Holly was frustrated about her mother's past. When Holly had talked about having to use the internet at the library, Maggie had grown quiet, silently eating the last of her brownie and looking out the window.

"Holly, your mom is doing really well now. You should be proud of her. It's not easy to give up something that's become a long-time addictive habit." Brigid noticed that Maggie was listening intently to the conversation.

"I know, and I am. I can't help it if I wished she'd done it a little sooner," Holly said as she turned and gave her mom a half smile.

"Don't think a day goes by that I don't regret it too, baby," Maggie said, putting her hand on her daughter's knee.

Brigid watched the two of them, wishing she could help in some way. She knew sometimes all people needed was a glimmer of hope. Brigid said, "I just had a thought. I was planning on going through my closets this weekend and getting rid of some things. I have a ton of clothes that I don't wear anymore. Would you like to go through the clothes before I donate them to the church and see is if there's anything that would work for you?" She paused as Holly and Maggie looked at each other.

"You don't have to take anything you don't like," Brigid continued. "I just really need to get rid of a lot of them. Most of them are from when I was working in Los Angeles, and they're too good to just throw away."

"Sure," Holly said after a moment. "That'd be great, thanks." She smiled at Brigid, realizing that she only wanted to help. She didn't think Brigid looked like she dressed in too mature of a style. Hopefully she could get a few new things, so she could get rid of some of her shirts that had holes in them.

"Great," Brigid said enthusiastically. "It's a win-win for everyone. I probably won't get to it until Sunday, though. I have a few things going on before then. Would it be okay if I bring them by here?" she asked.

Holly nodded. "Sure. Usually one of us is here. If not, leave them on the porch. And if you don't get to it, don't worry about it."

Brigid stood. "No, no. I'll do it for sure." She looked at her watch and said, "I've stayed here longer than I intended, so you probably need me to get out of your hair." She picked up her purse and seeing her cell phone in the side pocket made her think of another way she could help.

"By the way, if it's raining or bad weather and you have somewhere you need to go, call me." She pulled a slip of paper and a pen from her purse and wrote her number down. "If I can, I'd be happy to give you a ride." She handed the piece of paper to Maggie.

"You don't have to…," Maggie began. "You've done more than enough already."

"No really, it's fine. My work keeps me in the house all day. It's nice to have an excuse to get out once in a while." Brigid smiled. "Enjoy the rest of the brownies."

Brigid walked over to the door and let herself out. She climbed into her car and shut the door. *Such a bright young woman*, Brigid thought. *I hope she can find her way. I really would like to help both of them.* She started the car and headed home, feeling like she'd just made a couple of new friends.

She didn't know that only one of them would live long enough to become a friend.

CHAPTER THREE

Billy Watkins had started to move past the frustrated and heartbroken stage of his supposed "break-up" with Maggie and was now in the anger stage. He'd texted and called Maggie multiple times a day, all to no avail. He'd tried being sweet and loving at first. Then he'd begged her. Neither approach had worked. She wouldn't talk to him. It was like she'd flipped a switch.

One day, she'd been a fun-loving girl who was ready for anything and the next day she wanted to get clean and sober. She'd turned into the type of boring woman they used to make fun of together when they were high. The only time Maggie ever spoke to him now was when they ran into each other at the store or somewhere else in public, and he knew the only reason she said something was because she didn't have a choice.

A few times she'd even tried to act like she hadn't heard him call her name. It was only when he was able to stand in front of her that she acknowledged him, her good manners not allowing her to completely ignore him. Billy couldn't understand how she could end the relationship so suddenly and change so much in such a short space of time.

It all started when she decided to give up the life she'd been leading, an existence fueled by drugs and alcohol. It was nothing he wanted to do, and he couldn't understand why she was suddenly so set on the idea. Now that Mike had gotten busted, it had been almost impossible to find good meth, which is why he'd started going to Denver.

He knew a few people in Denver who could hook him up for a fair price. With the shortage in the Cottonwood Springs area, it had been very profitable for him. He'd told Maggie that he was making a lot of money. He knew she'd been worrying about money and was trying hard to make ends meet as a single mom, and now Billy was in a position to help her. That was the irony of the whole thing. He could help her, but she wouldn't have anything to do with him. It didn't make sense to him.

Billy was sitting on the dirty green recliner he loved so much which sat in the corner of his living room. It was where he did his best thinking. Next to it was an old wooden square end table with a cabinet at the bottom where he kept anything that was important.

All of his greatest ideas were born right in that spot. Of course, it was also where he'd been sitting when Maggie had told him she didn't want to see him anymore. He knew she was just confused, on a downer, and it wouldn't be long before she'd come crawling back to him. Billy was sure she still loved him.

Thinking about Maggie made him realize he couldn't remember the last time he'd brushed his teeth. He ran his hand across the top of his short, buzzed hair and sighed. Truth be told, as he looked down at his bare chest and dingy cargo shorts, he wasn't sure when he'd last taken a shower. He promised himself he'd do it later. He needed to take care of a few things first, like work on his car. There was a strange rattle that had been bugging him recently, and he needed to fix it.

The knock on the door startled him. He jumped, spun around, and silently crept to the window, so that he could peek outside to see who it was. He'd been getting the feeling someone was following him lately, and he was afraid it was the cops. He looked out the window and saw his friend, Samantha. Letting out the breath he didn't know he had been holding in, he walked over to the door and slid the deadbolt back before turning the knob.

"Hi, Billy," she said smiling. Her short curly blonde hair was flying everywhere in the breeze. She wore a loose pair of jeans and a black tank top.

"Hi, Sam," he said letting her in. "You scared the heck outta' me. I thought you were the cops, girl." Billy sighed and returned to his recliner, flopping down on it. He grabbed the remote and turned the TV on.

"Sorry," she said as she shut the door. She joined him in the living room and smoothed down the dirty sheet that was draped over the threadbare couch before sitting down on it. "How's it going?"

"I've gotta' make a run to Denver today," he said offhandedly. "My supply's getting low. I can't believe how much I've been moving now that word's gotten out. I probably won't go until later, though. Don't want to get there too early, you know." He paused and then said, "Maggie's still not answering my calls or texts."

"That's too bad," she said in a less than sympathetic tone of voice. She was secretly glad Maggie had flaked out on Billy. To Sam it meant Billy was now fair game. "What's her deal?" Every time she heard that Maggie wasn't answering his calls or texts, a flutter of excitement rose inside her. For months Sam had been hoping she and Billy could develop a serious relationship, but for some reason, he thought Maggie was special enough that he should wait until she came back him. Sam couldn't understand it.

"So, what's going on with you?" he asked, picking up the remote and surfing through the channels. He was still trying to come up with a way to get Maggie to listen to him. After all, he was the same guy he'd been the whole time they'd been together. She was the one who had changed. He didn't understand why she felt like she needed to break up with him now.

"I was just bored and thought I'd come over. There's nothing going on in the trailer park today. I was out for a walk and happened to come by here."

"Imagine that," he said distractedly as he continued to change the channels. He knew how life in the trailer park was and how everyone there gossiped about each other. He didn't care for Sam very much and the only reason Billy kept her around was because she could tell him what was going on at Maggie's. He wanted to make sure Maggie wasn't seeing anyone else. "By the way, did you see Maggie this morning?"

"No," Sam said, feeling deflated. She'd thought for a moment he was going to focus on her. "I haven't seen her since I talked to her at the store a week ago. She sounded crazy, in my opinion. I think something's wrong with her. Maybe she got abducted by aliens? I dunno'. She said she's started volunteering at the church."

"Seriously?" Billy said as he looked at Sam. He couldn't believe it. *What is happening to my beautiful girl?* he thought. The Maggie he knew had never set foot in a church and now she was volunteering in one? He had to find a way to get her back. She wasn't acting like herself at all. They used to laugh together about people who went to church all the time. He couldn't believe she'd become one of them, brainwashed by the God squad.

"Yeah, I guess she's been helping that Missy chick, you know, the priest's wife, keep the church clean and stuff like that. It's almost as if she worships the priest and his wife. You should have heard her going on and on about them. How they spend so much time helping people and they don't get paid for it. Blah, blah, blah. Honestly, I stopped listening after a little bit, because it was so boring. I don't even want to clean my house, so why would I want to clean someone else's? And the church? That place is huge." She shook her head. "No way, man."

"I gotta' get her back, Sam," Billy said as he looked at her. "I have to find out what she's getting over there that she isn't getting here with me." He looked around his little apartment and smiled. To him, it was great. He was oblivious to the uncleanliness and the sour odor that prevailed throughout. He lived on his own and didn't have a day job to worry about. He could sleep when he wanted, eat what he wanted, and do whatever he well pleased. It was beyond him why someone would volunteer for work they didn't need to do when they could laze around all day doing nothing.

"She told me she'd found God," Sam finally said. She spun around on the couch, so she could stretch her legs out. There was no place she felt quite as safe as when she was with Billy. His apartment was like a home away from home.

"God?" he asked incredulously. "You've got to be kidding me!" Billy scoffed and then laughed. He never imagined Maggie would become one of those people. He'd always thought she was an atheist, like he was. Billy couldn't remember a time he'd ever believed in God. To him, God was just an excuse people used because they didn't have what they wanted while they were on earth, so they thought it would be there for them in heaven. He only believed in the things he could see, and Heaven, Hell, and God were not on his radar.

"Billy, I didn't say I agreed with her. I'm just telling you what she said to me. She told me when she helps out and stays clean she feels closer to God, whatever that's supposed to mean." Sam leaned her head back and stared at the old '70's style popcorn ceiling. "I can't imagine it being any better than laying around eating jelly doughnuts."

"I can't believe she's getting all religious." The thought of someone turning away from him for comfort and turning to an invisible God enraged Billy. He had to take a few deep breaths to calm himself down.

He nervously paced back and forth across the thin carpet until the sound of a door shutting outside made him race to the window. Peeking through the blinds he saw it was just the old woman who lived next door. She was lugging in her groceries and pushed the door shut with her hip.

He turned away from the window and continued to pace around

the living room. Billy knew the situation with Maggie was serious. She'd gotten mad at him before, but she was usually over it after a day or two. She'd answer his call or text or even show up on his doorstep, acting as if nothing had happened. He should have known when she asked him to get clean with her that things were about to change. He just didn't know that he'd be the collateral damage in her transformation.

Billy remembered the day Maggie had told him she was breaking up with him. She'd come over ranting about Mike Loomis getting thrown in jail and that woman at the B & B getting murdered. He couldn't remember everything she'd said since he'd been high as a kite, but he kind of thought she'd said she was afraid of getting busted and losing her kid. She went on about how she couldn't imagine living without her "baby girl."

He didn't care for the scrawny kid with the saucer eyes, and he was pretty sure the feeling was mutual. She made a habit of disappearing whenever he showed up at Maggie's place, and if she did stick around, she always made him feel stupid about something he'd said. Billy couldn't stand it when people acted like they were smarter than him, just because they read books.

After that Maggie started talking about all the bad things she'd done and how she was afraid she was going to go to Hell when she died. She ranted about the money and other things she'd stolen, so she could buy drugs and alcohol. She was terrified that she'd die and the only thing she'd be remembered for was what a bad person she'd been.

He'd tried to lighten the mood by telling her he knew a few things she was really good at, but she didn't think that was very funny. That's when she'd told Billy she wanted him to get sober with her. He could barely keep a straight face when she'd said it. There was no way that was going to happen. What kind of a drug dealer doesn't do drugs? Added to that she wanted him to stop drinking beer? No, that was not an option. What else would he do when he was bored?

She'd stormed out of the apartment that night. Ever since then there had been absolute silence from Maggie. No phone calls. No texts. The more he thought about the way she'd acted, the more convinced he became that there was only one reasonable explanation. Maggie had to be seeing another guy.

Billy knew he wouldn't have any peace until he got to the bottom of it. He decided he'd sit outside Maggie's house, and even follow her if he had to. There was no way he'd let her leave him for another man. He'd done everything he could for her. Billy made the decision that if he couldn't have Maggie, no one would have Maggie.

He left Sam sitting on the couch in the living room and went to his bedroom, grabbed some clothes that smelled clean, and headed to the bathroom. While he was in the shower he decided that after he returned from the trip he had to make to Denver, he was going to find Maggie and demand some answers.

CHAPTER FOUR

All eyes were on the person on stage in charge of the award-giving.

"Our last award recipient has constantly shown such outstanding academic achievement that she continues to amaze her teachers, because she excels in everything she does. This next award doesn't get handed out very often, but it was created specifically for students like this one, students who not only get good grades, but master any challenge placed before them.

"They show hope and promise, despite any struggles or obstacles that may be in their path. They turn those obstacles into stepping stones used to achieve their goal, rather than allowing their focus to be broken. This year, I am extremely proud to hand out the District Honors Achievement Award to Miss Holly Lewis!" Principal Bartlett clapped loudly as the entire student body, with only a few exceptions, and teachers joined him in a long round of applause.

Holly couldn't believe what she'd just heard. She looked around in nervous amazement, seeing the eyes of her teachers and classmates on her. She smiled faintly as she stood up, unsure of herself with everyone watching her.

Don't trip, don't trip, don't trip, she mentally said to herself. She wasn't always the most graceful person, and now with the whole school staring at her, she was afraid she might do something embarrassing. She lowered her gaze to her black and white off-brand sneakers, paying very close attention to each step she took. Once she made it into the center aisle between the rows of students, she made the mistake of looking up.

The first thing she saw was Amanda and her two mean girlfriends, Morgan and April. Amanda had been picking on Holly since they'd been in kindergarten. It seemed that no matter what achievement Holly acquired, Amanda found some way to try and ruin it for her. Maybe it was the fact that no matter how hard she tried, Holly still got better grades than she did.

Amanda always came in second to the meek little blonde girl who sat in the back of the class, never drawing attention to herself. It wasn't as though Holly consciously tried to show her up. She just always did her best in every single class, and the problem was, Amanda's best was never as good as Holly's.

Holly took a deep breath and tried to put their faces out of her mind. She knew she wasn't as rich or as popular as they were, but academically, she always did better than Amanda. What Amanda didn't understand was that there was no way Holly would ever stop working hard in school.

It was the only way she knew of to avoid growing up and becoming like her mother. Her education was her ticket out of Cottonwood Springs and as far away from her mother as she could possibly get. Her goal was to leave the small town and everyone who had ever looked down their nose at her because of the things her mother did.

Holly slowly made her way up to the podium and then smiled at Principal Bartlett. He was a kind man, balding with greyish brown hair which formed a ring around his head. Today, the middle school principal was wearing a light blue dress shirt and a purple tie with a scowling yellow cartoon bird imprinted on it. Principal Bartlett and a handful of teachers were the only ones Holly would have good memories of once she left Cottonwood Springs. In many ways, they'd become her surrogate parents. Each one kept a friendly eye on her and helped her in any way they could.

"You've done very well, Holly. We're all very proud of you. We need to get a couple of photos for the school newspaper," the principal said as they posed on the stage for a photograph. When the photos had been taken, and as she returned to her seat, she saw Miss Baker smiling a big toothy grin at her. She was Holly's favorite teacher and perhaps the closest thing to a real mother she'd had the entire time she'd been in middle school. Miss Baker was a sixth-grade science teacher, and Holly often visited her during the lunch hour or after school.

Although Holly had a few friends, she preferred to keep them at a distance. Friends want to come over, have slumber parties, and do stuff like that. Holly didn't want anyone visiting the trailer. She couldn't risk anyone seeing her mom messed up or how rundown their home was. She was embarrassed about her whole living situation. After the awards assembly and school was over, Miss Baker approached Holly in the hallway.

"I'm so happy for you," she said with a smile. "That is really a very special honor."

Holly looked down at her feet, clearly uncomfortable with the praise. "Thanks," she said, "I was pretty surprised."

"I don't see why. You deserve it more than anyone," Miss Baker said. She always tried to praise Holly as much as possible. She had a feeling Holly didn't get much praise elsewhere. "Was your mother able to come to the assembly?" she asked as she looked around.

"No, she doesn't come to these things," Holly said with a frown. Her mother had never come to a single play, awards assembly, or parent teacher conference. It might have been the only thing Holly could count on her to do.

"I'm sorry to hear that. I bet once she sees your award, though, she'll be kicking herself for not coming."

"Probably," Holly said, but inwardly she doubted it. She knew she should have told her mother about the awards assembly, but she didn't. Although her mother was clean for now, Holly wasn't sure how long it would last. She hadn't wanted her mother to show up for the first time and be messed up. That would be even more embarrassing than being the kid whose mother never came to anything. It was bad enough that most kids knew her mom was a drunk and a druggie. They didn't need to see it first-hand.

"What are you going to do on your day off tomorrow?" Miss Baker asked. The following day, Friday, was an in-service day for teachers, but the students didn't have class.

"I'll probably end up going to the library or something," Holly said.

"By the way, have you had a chance to read the book I recommended to you?" Miss Baker asked. She was talking about one that she'd found at the library and thought Holly would like.

"Yes, I'm almost done with it. I'll probably finish it tonight," Holly said smiling. "It's really good. Thank you."

"I agree. I couldn't put it down," Miss Baker said. "Well, I'll let you go. Enjoy your three-day weekend and try to do some kid stuff. Everyone needs a break from studying once in a while." She smiled and waved as she walked away.

Holly turned back to her locker and began spinning the dial on the combination lock. *I'd love to be able to act like a kid,* she thought. *Instead I have to worry about adult stuff because my mom won't.* Opening the door of her locker, she slid her backpack off her shoulder, and began to switch out her books. She had some homework she needed to do over the weekend, so she wanted to make sure she had the books she would need.

Suddenly Holly was knocked off balance, her backpack dropped to the floor, and her papers and folders scattered onto the floor. A few kids who were standing nearby giggled, while others completely ignored her.

"Hey, watch where you're going!" Holly heard a voice say.

She looked up to see Amanda and her friends laughing and walking away. She'd purposely bumped into Holly, causing her to drop everything. With her papers scattered across the hallway, a few kids were nice enough to step over them, but most of them didn't care and simply walked on top of them.

Holly dropped to her knees and started to pick them up. She'd worry about organizing the mess later.

"Here, let me help you," a deep voice said. She looked up and saw Wade Taylor stooping down to help. He'd already changed into his baseball uniform for his after-school practice. His golden-brown hair glistened in the sunlight, beaming through the windows above the lockers. When he met her eyes, he smiled a lopsided grin that made Holly feel as though her heart had stopped. His piercing blue eyes were bright, and his face was deeply tanned.

"Oh, thanks anyway, but you don't have to," she said quickly. Although she really liked Wade, as in really, really liked him, she knew what would happen if Amanda saw him helping her. Amanda was always fawning all over Wade, but he didn't seem the least bit interested in her. That only seemed to infuriate her more, which in turn, made Holly like him even more.

"It's no trouble," he said as he handed her the last of her papers. "Actually, I wanted to talk to you. I was wondering if you could help me with something?"

Holly looked at him, clearly surprised. She'd talked to Wade from time to time when they were in class, and while he'd always been pleasant to her, she didn't think of the two of them as being friends. She wondered what he could possibly need her help with.

"I did really bad on our last science test. I was wondering if maybe you could tutor me or something? My parents would pay you for your time. You always know everything, and I thought maybe you could help me understand a few things." His bright, eager eyes left Holly speechless for a moment before she caught herself.

"Yeah, uh, sure. Not a problem. I'm actually planning on spending the day at the library tomorrow," she said. The last thing she wanted was for him to come to the trailer park. She was afraid if he saw where she lived, and if her mom was home, he'd start treating her like Amanda did.

"That's perfect," he said smiling again and showing his teeth which were incredibly white and straight. Holly remembered when he'd worn braces two years ago. Obviously, they'd been a success. His smile would melt anyone. "I'll see you tomorrow at the library, say… 10:30?"

Holly simply nodded, unable to muster a verbal response.

"Alright, I gotta' get to practice, but I'll see you tomorrow," he said with a smile and a wave, as he jogged down the hallway.

Oh my gosh, Holly thought. *I have a study date with Wade.* She shut her locker and hurried out of the school building, lost in her daydreams, and eager for tomorrow to come.

CHAPTER FIVE

When Billy pulled his car back into the parking lot of his apartment complex, Samantha Rogers felt like it was time for her to make her move. She'd ridden to Denver with Billy and enjoyed every minute of it. If anything, it just confirmed to her that they were supposed to be together. He was so smart and good-looking, she couldn't resist flirting with him.

Sam had always considered Maggie a friend, but Billy was more important to her. He was everything any woman could ever want. Sam couldn't understand why Maggie had left him. Oh well, even if she did want him back, it would be too late. He was a free man, and Sam had every intention of making it work to her advantage.

"Thanks for riding along with me tonight," Billy said as he turned off the car's engine.

"Thanks for taking me with you," she answered, smiling sweetly. "I had a great time."

They got out of Billy's old Cutlass and walked up to the door of his first-floor apartment. He unlocked it and pushed it open, so Sam could enter first. She relished the feeling of having him open the door for her as she stepped inside his apartment.

"I'll be back in a minute. Make yourself comfortable." Billy said as he walked down the dark hallway of the apartment and out of sight. In a moment, Sam heard the bathroom door close.

She looked around the living room and noticed there weren't any traces of Maggie. She hadn't left anything of hers at Billy's apartment, which Sam took as a good sign. The two of them had been together for quite some time, and Sam would have expected Maggie to have left something of hers in the apartment. She walked around in the living room and then looked towards the kitchen.

I'm not seeing a jacket, spare clothes, and I'm willing to bet there's not even a toothbrush in the bathroom, she thought to herself. *Maybe Billy wasn't all that invested in Maggie? She sure didn't seem to have been invested in him, that's for sure. Maybe it was just that she was something familiar to him. I wonder what would happen if someone else were to come along and make Billy feel extra special again?*

The more Sam thought about it the more certain she was that she was right. She only knew one way to get a man's full attention and make him feel special. Without a moment's hesitation, she quickly began to undress. By the time she heard the bathroom door open, she was posing naked out of sight from the hallway. She decided to stand to the side, so Billy would be surprised when he stepped into the room.

Sam held her breath as she heard his footsteps coming down the hall. "I don't know about you," he started to say, "but I think those burgers were…" Billy's sentence dropped as he came around the corner and saw her standing there in the nude.

Sam stepped forward and wrapped her arms around Billy. She pushed her mouth to his and moved her body against his. Billy dropped his hands to her hips for a moment and then gently pushed her away.

"What are you doing?" he asked as he took several steps backward, widening his distance from her.

"Billy, I want to be with you," Sam whispered in a low sultry voice.

"But I'm with Maggie," he said, still clearly flustered. "Come on now, Sam. Make yourself decent, so I can talk to you right." He turned and rushed into the kitchen where he began to fumble around.

Sam walked over to the couch where she'd put her clothes and began to put them back on. "I know you liked it," she said loudly. A moment later she said, "Alright, I'm dressed. You can come back in."

Billy walked into the living room, drinking a can of beer. "Sam, what in the devil were you thinking?" he asked as he moved towards his recliner. Sam grabbed her shoes and sat down on the couch.

"I'm thinking I want to spend more time with you," she said, keeping her eyes on him to gauge his reaction. "Doing things other than talkin'."

"I told you I'm with Maggie. How many more times do I have to say it?" Billy asked in an agitated voice.

"I know that, but I haven't seen her around here for quite a while now. You may think you're with her, but it sure looks to me like she's not very interested in being with you." Sam knew what she'd said was cruel, but she thought it was time Billy admitted Maggie wasn't coming back. The penny didn't seem to have dropped with him.

"No!" he said in a voice that was so loud and sharp it made Sam jump. "No," he said again, more calmly. "She's just got a wild streak in her. That's all. She'll be back soon." His eyes softened, and he looked directly at Sam. "It's not that I don't think you're pretty or anything, darlin', it's just that my heart belongs to Maggie. If she wasn't in the picture, maybe we'd have a future, but she is and always will be." He leaned back and took a big swallow of his beer.

"We don't have to tell her nothin'," Sam said trying one more time. She'd made her mind up to keep trying, no matter what he said about Maggie and him being together.

"Look, Sam, I'm really flattered. There's a lot of things I do that I probably shouldn't, but cheating isn't one of them. It's like the one thing I still hold on to. My dad cheated on my mom, and that's the reason they got divorced. I won't do that. Can you understand?" Billy asked, his eyes searching Sam's for a favorable response.

"Yeah, sure. I understand," she said dejectedly. "Well, I hope nobody snatches me up before you decide she's not coming back. If that happens, you just might lose your chance." Sam stood up and smoothed her blouse.

She walked over to the door, seductively wiggling her back side just in case Billy was still looking. She closed the door behind her and proudly walked around the corner of the building before allowing her shoulders to sag.

The fact she knew he was tempted helped a little, but her ego was still bruised by being turned down by him. She couldn't remember ever having had a man reject her physical advances. She knew she could get Billy if it wasn't for Maggie. *I know he desired me,* she told herself. *For a moment he kissed me back.*

It's all Maggie's fault, she thought. *He said if she wasn't in the picture he'd come after me. I just have to convince him she's not coming back. But it's already been weeks since she said she was done with him, and he still hasn't let go. How much longer is he willing to wait?*

It's time I moved things along, she decided. *Somehow, I need to make him see that she's out of his life, like forever. But how I am going to do that?*

She considered different ways she could prove to Billy that Maggie wasn't coming back. Maybe she could convince Maggie to move and then record her conversation with her. But even if Maggie moved, what if Billy followed her? Sam knew she didn't have enough money to follow him. She decided that was a bad idea, because then she'd be completely without Billy. She continued to think as she walked the four blocks to her home at the trailer park.

What if I could make her disappear? What if she ran away in the middle of the night? I could tell her I'd heard some people were out to kill her because of things she'd done in the past. I'd tell her that she couldn't let anyone know where she was going. She thought the idea had potential, but there were holes in the plan, like what if she came back?

I just have to make sure she leaves forever, Sam thought. Then it clicked. She didn't have to convince Maggie to go anywhere. All she had to do was kill Maggie, and she'd be gone for good. That would eliminate the problem of her ever returning. Maggie would be completely out of the picture and Billy would be hers, forever. Sam began to smile. As she rounded the corner and walked into the trailer park, she'd formed a plan.

CHAPTER SIX

Holly was standing in front of the library doors when the librarian unlocked them at 9:30 the next morning.

"Good morning, Holly," the librarian said.

"Good morning, Margaret," Holly responded. "How has your week been?"

"Wonderful, dear." Holly walked into the empty library which felt more like a home to her than the trailer did. The shelves filled with books were much more comforting to her than being in the tiny bedroom where she slept. Here she could escape into a different world, a world where she could be anything and anyone she wanted to be. At the trailer, she was her mother's daughter.

"Are you looking for anything special?" the older woman asked. Holly wished Margaret could have been the grandmother she'd never had. She could tell Margaret had been blonde when she was younger, before her hair had turned white, because she could see slight traces of blond mixed in with the white. Her friendly, lined face had never once scowled at Holly. She was pretty sure the older woman had figured out why she came to the library so often. There wasn't much that remained a secret in the small town of Cottonwood Springs.

After the first few times Holly checked out books in the morning, and then stayed there all day to read them, Margaret had introduced herself. She'd invited Holly to the employee's lounge where she shared tea and cookies with her, and they'd become friends.

Holly often helped Margaret with the simple duties around the library. Reshelving the books back into their rightful places had been the main chore she performed. Holly couldn't stand it when she found books laying around in odd places, and Margaret reciprocated by bringing in snacks to share with Holly.

Holly left the books she was returning on the counter, so Margaret could check them in when she got a chance. She wandered through the stacks of books looking for ones that were out of place, killing time while she waited for her meeting with Wade. It wasn't until after she'd gotten home yesterday that she remembered he'd said his parents would pay her for helping him.

As far as she was concerned, spending time with Wade would be payment enough, but she couldn't afford to turn the money down. Her shoes were getting worn down from all the walking she did. Part of her thought she should tell her mom about Wade and being paid to help him, but she was afraid her mother would think Holly felt she had to earn money because she couldn't properly support her daughter. Holly didn't want to put any additional stress on her. She didn't want to have to hand the money over to her mom either, in case her mom used it for drink or drugs.

Holly picked out a few books she thought might help Wade. They'd been studying cells in science class recently, so she guessed that was probably what he needed help with. She pulled out her favorite books on the subject and put them on the table she usually occupied in the back corner of the main room in the library.

"Hey, Holly," she heard a familiar voice say. Looking up she saw Wade crossing the library floor to where she was sitting.

"Hey, yourself," she said smiling. He was wearing a black baseball cap, a Colorado Rockies baseball jersey, a black jacket, and a pair of jeans that looked like they were new.

"I came here early hoping I'd beat you, but obviously I didn't get here soon enough." He dropped his backpack on a chair before sitting in the one beside it.

"Yeah, I got here just as they opened this morning. I was bored." Actually, getting to the library when it first opened was one of her favorite things to do, but she didn't think girls that Wade would be interested in would find that their favorite thing to do, so she didn't mention that part.

"That's cool," he said, digging in his backpack. He pulled out a sealed envelope and slid it across the table to her. "That's from my parents as payment. I have no idea how much they put in there, and I don't want to know. Please, don't open it until later." He had a pained expression on his face.

"Why?" she asked as she put it in her pocket.

"Because the larger the amount of money they gave you, the more hopeless they must think I am. They've both tried to help me, but it hasn't worked. They finally told me to find a classmate who'd be willing to tutor me. If they gave you a decent chunk of cash, that means they probably think I'm a lost cause, and I'm going to stress you out," he said with a nervous laugh. He pulled off his cap and pushed a wayward chunk of hair out of his eyes, only for it to fall right back down again.

"Wade, don't worry. I'll stick around however long it takes for you to get it."

"Good, because it may take a while," he said.

"It doesn't matter how long I stay here at the library. My mom won't miss me," Holly said, although it hurt her to say it.

Wade was silent for a moment, and then he said, "I heard she's doing better. Is that true?" He'd said it softly, as though he was afraid to ask.

Holly's eyes shot up, fear gripping her, before she realized he hadn't meant anything bad by what he said. She nodded. "Yeah, so far."

"Good," was all he said.

Holly picked up one of the books she'd selected and began working with Wade. Over the next couple of hours, they studied for a while, took a break, and then studied some more. Since they were in the same grade, they'd known each other their entire lives. Growing up in Cottonwood Springs, it was pretty hard not to know all of one's peers.

"I really appreciate you doing this," Wade said on one of their breaks. "You're probably saving my baseball career."

"Oh, I don't know about that," Holly said modestly.

"No, I mean it. After our mid semester grade cards came out, I thought I was toast. Coach got ahold of me and told me if I was still failing science at the end of the year I couldn't play on the team anymore." He leaned back and sighed. "It's not like I can just go to some other team. Since there aren't any other school baseball teams around here, my options are pretty limited."

"Honestly, Wade, it's no trouble at all." She pulled the envelope out of her pocket and pushed it across the table to him. "And your parents don't need to pay me. I don't mind. I enjoy helping you, and I'd be here anyway."

He put his hand over hers and stopped her. "No, keep it. You deserve every cent they gave you and probably more." He smiled. Their eyes met a moment before he realized he was still holding her hand. He blushed and quickly pulled it back.

Holly looked away. She didn't want to read too much into the gesture. She looked around the room, trying to distract herself, so she wouldn't look embarrassed. She saw a familiar face and tried to remember where she knew the woman from.

"Hi, Holly," the woman said, waving to her. She noticed the woman's vivid red hair and remembered she was the woman who'd made the amazing brownies and driven her mom home the other night.

"Hi, Brigid," she said, waving back at her.

Brigid walked over to their table and smiled. "What are you two up to?"

"I'm just helping Wade study some stuff from our science class," Holly said gesturing towards her companion.

He nodded. "She's really great at it, too. For the first time, it's actually starting to make sense to me."

Brigid looked at the books and grimaced. "Science, huh? I'd be lost, too. I never was any good at it." She smiled at them. "Well, I'll leave you alone, so you can finish your studies. I'm just here returning a few books. Enjoy the rest of the day." She smiled and walked away.

"How do you know Brigid?" Wade asked after she'd left.

"I met her when she drove my mom home. Do you know her?" Holly asked.

"No, not exactly, but when that lady who owned the B & B was murdered, I remember reading that she was the one who helped catch the person who'd committed the crime."

"Really?" Holly said with surprise in her voice. Looking at Brigid, you sure wouldn't think she was a crime-solving kind of lady. She looked too posh for that.

Wade shrugged, "I don't know any more than what I read in the paper. It had a picture of her and everything."

Holly turned around and looked at Brigid as she stood at the library counter. It made her see the woman in a whole new light.

When she'd brought her mother home from her meeting, Holly had thought Brigid was some rich person trying to do a good deed for the poor people in town, kind of something to make her realize just how good she had it. The thought she might actually be a good person who truly wanted to help people made Holly pause and reconsider.

"Wow," Holly said. "That's pretty cool."

"Yeah, they even had her dog in the picture. I guess he helped catch the person by jumping on them and holding them down." Wade dug in his backpack and pulled out two granola bars. "Here," he said tossing her one.

"That's crazy," Holly said in awe as she caught the granola bar.

"I know. Didn't you see it on the news?" he asked as he bit into his bar.

"We don't have a TV," she said quietly, peeling off the wrapper.

"Oh," he said a little flustered. "Really?"

"Well, we have a small one, but we don't have cable," she explained.

"What do you play video games on?" he asked, clearly surprised.

"Uh, I don't," she said feeling embarrassed. *Now he's going to realize how poor I am*, she thought, *and he won't want to be around me anymore.*

"Dang," he said. He was quiet for a moment and then he said, "Why don't you come over to my house when we're done? We can play video games or just hang out and watch TV." He smiled. "I think my mom has a pizza in the deep freeze and a bunch of other snacks. Want to?"

Holly sat in shock for a moment before she collected herself. "That sounds great, Wade. Thanks."

CHAPTER SEVEN

Brigid's cell phone buzzed with a text as she was brushing her hair. When she picked it up she saw it was from Linc.

Almost back home. They're in a good mood.

Linc had left earlier to pick up his parents at the Denver airport. He and Brigid had made plans to have dinner at Linc's house after they'd had a chance to spend a little time with him. Linc was making an Italian style pot roast which he'd started in his slow cooker before he'd left for Denver. He told Brigid he'd do the finishing touches on it when he got back.

After Brigid left the library, she'd gone shopping for a new dress to wear that evening. She wanted to make a good impression on Linc's parents, and she hadn't liked anything she'd seen in her closet that morning. She'd settled on a floral wrap dress with a soft deep blue background.

She took one last look in the mirror, pleased with her makeup, the new dress, and the way her hair had turned out. She walked into the great room where Jett was in his customary place on his loveseat. "You about ready to head over to see Linc?" Brigid asked the big dog. Jett raised his head as soon as he heard Linc's name. "Yeah, I thought so," she said smiling.

Brigid debated whether they should walk to Linc's house or drive, but then she remembered rain was forecast for the evening, and it was already clouding up. "I think we better err on the safe side and take the car," she said to Jett. "If you got wet on the way home, I'd be smelling wet dog all night long, and that doesn't particularly appeal to me." Jett woofed, seemingly in complete agreement with Brigid. After they walked out the front door, Jett waited patiently beside her as she opened the back door for him. A few minutes later, they pulled into Linc's driveway.

"Jett, I want you to be on your best behavior. We want to make a good impression on Linc's parents," Brigid said turning towards him before getting out of the car. "No funny business." Jett started panting with excitement when he realized they had arrived at Linc's house, but to Brigid, it almost looked like a smile.

They walked towards the front door, but before they could ring the doorbell, Linc opened it. "Brigid, Jett, you're just in time." He greeted Brigid with a chaste kiss on the cheek.

A moment later Linc introduced Brigid and Jett to his parents, James and Marilyn Olson. They laughed at how big the dog was and began to pet him, cooing over how well behaved and sweet he was. It was apparent Jett was enjoying being the center of attention.

"He's a really great dog," Brigid said. "I'm so glad I adopted him."

Marilyn Olson was a small woman with dyed blonde hair. She didn't look her age and moved and acted as though she was only slightly older than her son. Brigid noticed that Linc and Marilyn shared the same shape of nose and even their cheekbones, but even though Linc shared some facial traits with his mother, it was his father, James, who he most resembled. The two men were the same height and roughly the same build, although the older man didn't stand quite as straight as his son did.

"I'm so glad you were able to stop here and see Linc," Brigid commented as they sat down at the long wooden dinner table. "Where were you visiting?"

"We're on our way back from a trip to New York. We decided to go there for our anniversary," Marilyn smiled. "It was even better than I'd imagined. It's quite different from Arizona."

"I've never been to New York, so I can only imagine." Linc appeared and poured everyone a glass of wine. Brigid lifted her glass and took a sip. "I really would like to go there someday."

"Maybe Linc will take you sometime. After living there for so long, he knows it pretty well," James said with a wink.

"Well, if he's anything like his father, it may take a long time," Marilyn said with a laugh.

During dinner which consisted of an Italian pot roast served over noodles, butternut squash soup, Italian herb bread, and the cream cheese brownies Brigid had brought for dessert, they talked about this and that. Jett was stretched out under the table, hoping one of them would drop a crumb, either accidentally or on purpose.

Brigid began to relax, realizing that James and Marilyn were very likable down-to-earth people. There was nothing false or showy about them. They were who they seemed to be, and that was that. After the way her ex-husband's family had been, Linc's parents were a breath of fresh air.

"I don't know about all of you, but I'm stuffed. That was excellent, Linc, and Brigid, thank you for the brownies," James said as he stood up and began clearing the table.

"Dad, you don't have to do that," Linc said, standing up to help him.

"Sit down, son. Your mother has trained me well. You cooked a wonderful meal, and you're letting us spend the night here. Carrying the dishes into the kitchen is the least I can do." When he was finished he said, "I'd love a cigar, and I remember that Linc doesn't like me to smoke in the house. Marilyn, let's go sit out on the back porch. Brigid, would it be okay if Jett joins us? He reminds me a lot of a dog Linc's brother had when the boys were growing up. I'd love to spend a little time with him."

"Of course, I think he'd like that," Brigid said. James called the dog who happily hopped up and joined his new friends as they went outside.

When he heard the glass door to the back patio being shut, Linc turned to Brigid. "They seem to really like you," he said.

"I hope so, because I sure like them. I don't understand how your ex-wife could have had problems with your parents." Brigid couldn't fathom anyone not getting along with the easygoing couple.

"Well, you'd have to understand what she was like, not exactly a warm fuzzy person. She was very superficial and thought my parents were too rough around the edges for her. I don't like to admit it, but she was a snob. She hated anything rural, which was why I always ended up skiing and doing things like that on my own."

"Forgive me for asking, but why did you marry her? She sure doesn't sound like she was very compatible with you." Brigid couldn't understand how Linc could have ever been with a woman like that. He seemed so outdoorsy and rugged, and there was nothing superficial about him.

"I honestly don't know, Brigid. I guess the best answer is that I was young and didn't really know who I was at the time. As I got older, I became determined to do the things that I loved, which turned me into the man you see today," Linc said with a shrug.

"Well, I like the guy I see today." Brigid placed her hand on his. "Thank you for inviting me over to meet your parents."

"And thank you for agreeing to meet them," he said. "I have to admit I was terrified to ask you."

"I'm sorry you were concerned," she said. "Not only do I like you, I like what we have together. If something comes up, we'll figure it out as we go. Life's too short for anything else. I just don't want to overly complicate it."

Linc paused, listening to the music that had been playing in the background. He raised a finger, "Is that…?" he continued to listen. "It is!" He jumped up and hurried over to the kitchen where he had his phone plugged in playing background music. After turning up the sound, he came back to Brigid and held out his hand. "May I have this dance?" he asked in a formal tone of voice.

Brigid laughed and took his hand. "Why, of course."

Linc pulled her into his arms and began to sway with the music.

"What is this song?" Brigid asked, listening to the blues song.

"You obviously don't listen to blues, do you?" Linc asked as they moved together in the area between the kitchen and the dining room. It was a wide-open area that echoed the music well. Brigid shook her head.

"It's called 'I'm Your Hoochie Coochie Man' by Muddy Waters," he began. "I first heard it a long, long time ago, and I've loved it ever since. It's been redone a number of times by more well-known artists. Some people think it actually influenced the way music is done today."

"Really?" Brigid had never really listened much to blues, but she had to admit the lyrics of the song were catchy. She found herself wanting to sway with the sound as it filled the room. The music, Linc's arms wrapped around her, and the heady smell of his cologne made Brigid feel as though she was dancing on air. She felt Linc's fingers begin to slide up and down her spine, gently caressing her. Looking up into his eyes, she saw a softness there. No expectations, no pressure. Just a complete and total fondness for her. Brigid felt herself melt just a bit inside at the thought of someone feeling that way toward her.

As the song ended, they stopped swaying to the music and simply held onto each other. Linc lowered his lips to Brigid's and kissed her. Not in the same way they'd kissed before. No, this time it felt different. As their mouths melded together, it was almost as if they were wrapping themselves in the other person. Getting lost in those places that had yet to be explored.

The next song on the playlist was a much more upbeat tune. Linc released Brigid, so that he could go turn the music volume back down. "Thank you for the dance," he said. There was a charge in the air that neither one of them could deny.

"Thank you for asking," she said, feeling her face redden. *What is this all about?* she thought. *I'm too old to blush like a young teenage girl. Especially since we've been seeing each other for several months now.*

"Alright, alright boy." They heard James' voice as the back door opened. "Hold your horses."

Jett came scrambling into the house, rushing over to Brigid's side. "What's wrong?" she asked as she bent over and began to scratch the big dog's ears.

Marilyn, who was right behind James, stepped into the kitchen and shut the door. "You should have seen it," she said with a laugh. "We were sitting out there in the dark, just enjoying the nighttime noises when this owl flew up and landed on a branch nearby. Jett was interested in it until it started hooting," Marilyn said, laughing harder. "And then it scared the dickens out of him, and he went scrambling towards the house."

James laughed loudly and slapped his knee, "I've never seen anything like it. I feel sorry for the poor guy, but it was still hilarious to watch." He walked over to Jett and patted his head. "It's alright, Jett. That mean old owl won't hurt you." He looked up at Linc and Brigid. "I think we're going to head off to bed. We've got a bit of jet lag. It was wonderful meeting you, Brigid. Will we see you tomorrow morning before we leave?"

She turned and looked at Linc who shrugged as if to say, "Up to you."

"Yes, I can come over," she said turning back to James.

"Wonderful," James said. "I'll cook breakfast for everyone. Why don't you bring Jett, too?" The older man nodded to her, as both James and Marilyn said their goodnights.

"I think it's time Jett and I should probably be going home, too," Brigid said, as Linc began rinsing plates and loading them in the dishwasher.

"You don't have to," he said drying his hands on a dish towel and turning around. He walked over to Brigid and put his hands on her hips. "You could always spend the night here."

"With your parents just down the hall?" she asked incredulously. "Are you crazy?"

"Well, it's not like we're teenagers," he said as he kissed her.

"That's true, but I wouldn't feel right…" she began.

"I never said we had to do anything." He smiled. "I just want to hold you tonight."

Brigid was tempted, but it didn't seem appropriate to her. Not with his parents under the same roof. "Sorry, I just wouldn't feel comfortable," she said in a decisive manner.

"Your call," he said kissing her again, "but you can't blame a guy for trying. By the way, you look gorgeous tonight. I love the dress."

"Thanks. You don't look so bad yourself."

He looked down at his dark maroon dress shirt with the sleeves rolled up and black slacks. "These old things? I just threw them on," he said with a laugh.

"Why don't you let me help you clean up the rest of this before we leave?"

"No, I've got it," he said returning to the sink and continuing to rinse the dinner dishes.

"Well in that case, I better get Jett home before he decides he's tired and won't get back up. We both know it's impossible to move him once he's down for the night. What time would you like us to come over in the morning?" Brigid asked as she collected her things.

"Dad usually gets up around 6:00," Linc said. "So around 6:30 will probably be good. I know you get up early, too, so I assume that's not a problem. Work for you?"

"We'll be here," she said. She walked over to him and bumped her hip against his. "I better go, but Linc, I have to tell you how cute you would look in an apron. There's nothing sexier than a man who does the dishes."

"I'll remember that," he said, grinning. "Just an apron?"

CHAPTER EIGHT

Frank Sterling sat in his recliner reading a book about caring for aged parents. He never thought he'd be in this position, but here he was. He looked across the living room at his father who was sitting in his wheelchair watching Wheel of Fortune. The old man had really gone downhill in the last few years. Ever since that woman, Maggie Lewis, had come into his life. Just thinking about her made his blood boil.

When his father was still living in his own home, he'd hired people to help him out as part of the disability care he received. After the first woman had to quit because she'd had a baby and needed more hours, Frank's dad had hired Maggie. At first things were going really well. She kept his dad's house clean, prepared his meals, and overall did a very good job, but then things went downhill. Frank began to notice that things were missing.

His father, Paul, had explained the missing things away by telling Frank that he was trying to get rid of all the excess things he'd accumulated over the years. "I don't need all this stuff," Paul had said. "The time has come to get rid of it. I'm not going to be around forever, you know."

Frank hadn't thought very much about it after their conversation. He wasn't overly concerned, because the things weren't valuable or of interest to him, such as an old lawnmower and various decorative items. For a while, Frank believed what his father had said, that he was just clearing things out. He'd done the same thing himself from time to time.

It all changed the afternoon he visited his father and noticed that his mother's favorite crystal vase was gone. That was when he knew something was very, very wrong. The vase had always been next to his deceased mother's picture, because she'd treasured it. Frank's mother and father had received it as a wedding gift from her great-grandmother. Frank knew there was absolutely no way his father would have gotten rid of it.

"I'm not sure what happened to it," his father had responded when Frank asked him what happened to it. "Are you sure it wasn't just moved to another table?" The old man was clearly confused, and Frank hadn't wanted to upset him, so he hadn't pushed it.

After that, every time Frank visited his father, he looked around to see what was still in his father's house. And every time, he noticed that something else was gone. A lot of the things his father no longer needed had been put away in the attic for safekeeping, so he wasn't sure if some of the missing items were up there. He had no plausible reason to go up there, so he hoped that the help had put things up there. But when Frank went into his father's office and looked at the checkbook that was on his father's desk, he knew something serious was amiss.

"Maggie told me MediCorp had been running late paying her," his father had said when Frank asked him why he was writing checks to Maggie. "From time to time I gave her some money just to help her out. She told me she'd deposit the money back into my account."

Maggie had never made a deposit to Paul's bank account, instead, she'd bled his father dry. Frank had no choice but to move his father in with his wife and him and sell his father's home. Unfortunately, by then Paul had dementia, and it had worsened to the point he was withdrawn and barely able to care for himself. He wouldn't eat or bathe unless forced to. He became confined to a wheelchair and barely spoke to anyone. Paul had lost the will to live.

Frank was reading the paper while Paul, staring at the television set, began to cough uncontrollably, saliva dripping from his lower lip. Frank rushed over to his father and pulled a handkerchief out to wipe off his father's chin. He looked at his watch and decided, even though it was a little early, he could give his father his next dose of medicine. He sighed as he walked over to the counter to get his father's pillbox.

If that woman hadn't taken almost all of dad's money, I could afford to find a nice nursing home for him, Frank thought. *Instead, I have to sit here and watch him slowly die.*

He took two pills out of the case and poured a small glass of juice. He walked over to where his father was and said, "Time for your medicine, Dad." He held out the pills and the cup of juice. The old man looked up at him as if wondering who Frank was and why he was giving him pills. Paul finally popped the pills in his mouth and washed them down with a drink of juice. Frank took the glass from him and walked back to the sink. He rinsed the glass out and put it in the dish drain.

Frank had tried to have Maggie arrested for stealing, but since his father had signed the checks, the sheriff had just shrugged his shoulders and apologized, explaining that there wasn't much he could legally do.

His wife, Eve, had taken it all in her stride. She did her best to help take care of the older man, but most of the caregiving fell on Frank's shoulders. After all, it was his father, not hers. As time went on, it became more and more stressful for both of them. He and Eve barely saw each other. She had to switch to working nights at their store, while he worked days. It was the only thing they could do, because someone had to be with Paul around the clock, but it wasn't easy on either of them.

Frank opened one of the kitchen cabinets and took out a can of beef stew for Paul's dinner. He didn't know how much longer he could keep all this up. What made it even worse was knowing Maggie Lewis was out there running around without a care in the world.

She'd ruined his father's life, and Frank was worried that the situation might ruin his own marriage. He didn't understand how the woman could live with herself.

He'd heard rumors about other things that she'd done, but they were just that, rumors. Nobody seemed to know if there was any truth to them. And those who did know wouldn't admit that they'd been taken advantage of by Maggie Lewis and made to look like a fool.

Frank understood how they felt. He didn't feel like telling everyone she'd swindled his dad out of a lot of money. Instead, he and Eve told people they felt it was an honor to be able to care for the ailing man and make sure he was treated well in his last years. In reality, they were caring for him because they couldn't afford to put him in a nursing home. He knew the resentment he felt about looking after his father, whom he loved dearly, was wrong, but it was eating him up inside.

As he was opening the can of stew and putting it into a bowl to heat in the microwave, Frank felt his ever-present anger boiling up to the surface. He knew Maggie had hurt countless people. The only thing she deserved was to be in as much pain as the people she'd hurt. And now that she'd supposedly turned over a new leaf, how come she got all the kindness and forgiveness, when those she'd swindled were left to deal with the consequences of her wrongdoing? It wasn't fair.

He put the bowl in the microwave, set the timer, and then walked over to the window in the back door and looked out. The sun was slipping behind the mountains, turning the sky dark blue. He couldn't stop thinking about Maggie. She needed to pay for what she'd done. She'd been responsible for his father's decline and taken away Frank and Eve's happiness. The only thing she deserved was for someone to do the same to her.

Looking out the window, it was as if a bolt of lightning had struck him and planted an idea in his mind. "That's exactly what she deserves," he whispered to himself, "for someone to put an end to her." He became so lost in his thoughts he didn't even hear the microwave beeping, letting him know his father's beef stew was ready.

CHAPTER NINE

The next morning Brigid was up bright and early, much earlier than was usual for her. If she was being honest with herself, she couldn't remember the last time she'd gotten up this early. She wanted to take a shower and be fresh before she went to Linc's house. Looking back on the evening before, she felt it had really been successful. She'd liked his parents, and they seemed to like her. It made her feel a bit more confident in her relationship with Linc. She knew at her age she probably shouldn't care, but even so, she was glad.

She pulled her hair back in a loose bun and put on a pair of black leggings and a tunic. When she returned from Linc's house she planned to go through her closet. She'd already taken a quick look and found a number of things she felt Maggie's daughter, Holly, would look great in.

"Ready to go, Jett?" Brigid asked as she walked into the great room. In response he bounded off of his loveseat and met her at the front door. A few moments later they walked through the front door of Linc's house.

"Good morning," Linc said giving her a quick kiss.

"And good morning to you," she said with a smile. "It smells wonderful in here."

"That's because Dad went all out this morning. I think he's trying to impress you," Linc whispered as he led her to the kitchen.

"Good morning, Brigid, Jett," James said as they entered the kitchen.

"Hello," she said warmly. "I don't know what you're cooking, but it smells wonderful."

Jett woofed in response to James' greeting.

"Good. We're having pancakes, eggs, and a bacon quiche Lorraine. There's also milk or orange juice, or both."

"Let me fix your plate," Linc said. "There's this special way Dad likes us to eat our eggs and pancakes. The eggs have to be on top of the pancakes, and you can't put the maple syrup on until the eggs have been eaten. He started doing it when we were kids as a way to get us to eat eggs, and it hasn't changed after all these years. The quiche is an old family favorite. Dad got up earlier than usual to make it this morning." He took a plate from the cabinet.

"It sounds wonderful," Brigid said, smiling.

"Go ahead and sit down. What would you like to drink?" Linc asked. "In addition to the milk and orange juice, there's coffee, and of course, water.

"I'll have orange juice, please," she said as she joined Marilyn at the table.

They greeted each other and a moment later Brigid looked over her shoulder at the men and said, "I could definitely get used to this."

"It's an Olson man thing," Marilyn said as she sipped her coffee. "They love to cook."

The two women chatted while the men served them breakfast. For the next few minutes, everyone was quiet, simply enjoying their breakfast.

"James, this quiche is fantastic. I'd love to have the recipe, if you're inclined to share it," Brigid said as she took her last bite of it.

"I'd consider it an honor and it's about the easiest thing in the world to make. When we're finished with breakfast, I'll write it down for you. I've made it so often, I know the recipe by heart."

"Thank you, and I definitely will be making it. My sister would love it."

When they were finished, Marilyn and Jim took turns telling funny stories about Linc when he was young. Although Linc laughed, Brigid could tell he was embarrassed.

"Your parents are a lot of fun. I loved the stories about you when you were young," Brigid told Linc as she was helping him clean up the breakfast dishes. James and Marilyn had left the kitchen to pack, since it was almost time for Linc to drive them back to the airport in Denver.

"I've never seen them so excited," he finally said. "They must really like you to tell you all those stories. And to think Dad made his special quiche just for you. That's impressive." He looked at her fondly. "I don't know why I was so nervous about you meeting them."

"Me neither," Brigid said as she handed him the last plate. "I'll say goodbye to your parents, and then Jett and I are going to head out. I need to go through my closet and clean it out."

"Oh?" Linc asked. "What for?"

"I met this mother and daughter who are struggling financially. I told them they could have some clothes of mine that I never wear to freshen up their wardrobe. They're roughly the same size as I am. I think I'll ask Fiona, too. She may have some stuff she's ready to get rid of. It's always so much easier to get rid of things when you know they're going to worthy people," Brigid said with a sigh.

"That's extremely generous of you. Let me know if you need any help with it," he said.

"I will." She turned and kissed him on the cheek. She heard suitcases being pulled down the hall, and a few minutes later she met his parents in the great room and smiled at them. "Jett and I are going to leave now," she said. "I'm so glad I got to meet you."

Marilyn and James hugged her. "We're glad we had a chance to meet you, and Jett, too," Marilyn said. She leaned in and whispered, "We need someone to keep an eye on Linc for us." She winked for emphasis.
"I heard that, Mom," Linc said as he walked into the room.

Brigid waved and said her goodbyes while they said goodbye to Jett. She stepped out the door and into the cool morning air, sorry to see them go.

****

By lunchtime, Brigid had gone through her closet and felt good about what she'd gotten rid of. From the looks of it, she thought she'd probably gotten rid of almost half of her wardrobe. Two trash bags, completely filled, sat on her bed, ready to go. She'd also thrown in a few purses she hadn't used in a while. She had a habit of keeping the old ones for "just in case." She hated to admit it, but "just in case" had never come. It seemed like a good time to let them go.

Amazingly, her stomach began to growl. She didn't know how her body could think it was hungry after such a big breakfast. She pulled out her phone to text her sister. She'd texted Fiona earlier, asking if she had any clothes she wanted to donate to a worthy cause. She knew Fiona didn't open the bookstore until later on Saturdays, so Brigid thought she'd probably had time to go through her closet earlier that morning.

She looked at her phone and saw that Fiona had texted her back.

Found quite a bit I could let go of. I'll take it to the shop with me. You can swing by whenever to pick it up.

Brigid smiled. She knew she could count on her sister. She sent a quick text in reply.

I'll be over in a little while. Have you eaten lunch yet?

Brigid sat down on her bed and waited while she watched the bubble on her cell phone appear, telling her that Fiona was replying to her text.

Not yet. If you bring me something good, I'll pay you back.

Brigid shook her head and laughed. Shoving her phone in her purse, she slung it over her shoulder before carrying the trash bags to the front door. Jett jumped up anxiously, ready to go with her.

"Not this time, Jett. You stay home and guard the house," she said as she opened the door. Jett stopped and looked at her with big sad puppy dog eyes before returning to the bone he'd been gnawing on. Brigid walked out the door, amused by how well a dog could communicate with a human without using any words.

After a quick stop at the local pizza place, Brigid drove through town toward her sister's bookstore, Read It Again. The smell of the piping hot pizza filled her car and made her stomach growl again, demanding to be fed. By the time she walked through the door of the bookstore with it, she was more than ready to eat.

"Good, you brought a pizza. Smells wonderful," Fiona said as she hopped off her stool behind the counter. Looking like she'd stepped out of some fashion magazine, she disappeared in the back of the store, returning with two paper plates. "Let's sit over there." She motioned to a pair of chairs in the corner. There was a low, round wooden coffee table in front of the chairs that was covered by magazines. Fiona pushed them out of the way, so they'd have room for the pizza.

Fiona loved food, but she loved her size two figure more. She allowed herself one-half of one piece of pizza. When they were finished eating and the leftovers had been stored in the small refrigerator in the back room, Fiona's curiosity got the better of her.

"Brigid, you never told me who these clothes are going to."

"They're mainly for the daughter of a woman I met while I was helping Missy at the church a couple of nights ago. She's trying to stay sober but having a teenage daughter in need of a new wardrobe isn't helping." Brigid said.

"I can understand that," Fiona nodded. "So, who's getting sober? Anyone I know?"

"Probably. She's lived in Cottonwood Spring her whole life. Her name's Maggie Lewis," Brigid said.

"Nice, Sis. You could have done a lot better," Fiona said.

"She mentioned she'd done some bad things. That bad, huh?" Brigid said, wincing.

"Uh, yeah. I'll bet you don't know the half of it, and with a mother like her, the kid doesn't have a chance," Fiona said looking at her sister. "Watch yourself with that woman. Don't invite her to your house is all I'm saying." She held her hands up in surrender to add emphasis to her words.

Brigid nodded. "I hear you. Like I said, I'm trying to help the daughter more than anything. Apparently, she's really smart and has a lot of potential. She's been getting picked on by some girls at school because she wears used clothes that came from the church. You know how eighth grade girls are. It's only going to get worse next year in high school."

"Ain't that the truth," said Fiona rolling her eyes. "Well, I'm glad to hear the girl isn't like her mother, because I've heard some stories you wouldn't believe." Fiona reached into her purse and took out a cigarette. "I know, I know, my pure older sister doesn't like me to smoke, but it's my shop and I love one after I've eaten."

"Okay, just don't blow smoke in my direction. Back to Maggie Lewis. What kind of stories have you heard about her?" Brigid asked as she pulled her feet up into the chair, tucking her legs beneath her, and waving her hand in front of her face, making sure that none of Fiona's cigarette smoke got close to her.

"I don't know how true all of them are. I just overhear things when locals come in here, you know? But I heard she worked for Paul Sterling before he went downhill. He had that disability thing where they pay people to come to your house and help out, like a caretaker.

"He ended up hiring her, and from what I understand, it was great at first. But after a while, it seems some household things began to come up missing. At first Paul explained to his son, Frank, that he was just getting rid of old junk that was gathering dust. But after more time passed Frank noticed things missing that his father never would have gotten rid of. Paul explained it away by saying they were probably up in the attic being stored, but they were gone."

"Maggie was telling him she was putting things in the attic and stealing them instead?" Brigid asked incredulously.

"I guess so," Fiona shrugged. "About that time Frank found out she'd been getting Paul to write checks to her under the pretense she'd pay the money back directly into his account. Only she never did."

"Oh, man." Brigid was having a hard time imagining the kind woman she'd given a ride home to swindling an old man out of his money. Yet, she knew drugs could make even the best person turn into a monster. It broke her heart to think of poor Paul Sterling getting robbed right under his nose and in his own home by his caretaker.

"Yep. That's why Frank had to move his dad in with them. There wasn't much money left. I don't know the details. All I know is Frank had to sell his father's house and move him into his home."

"Is that all you've heard about her?" Brigid hated to ask, but she felt she needed to know what this woman was capable of, just in case she had more dealings with her. She wondered if Missy knew about any of this.

"Well, I've also heard something that seems possible, but I don't know for sure. I heard someone say she was seeing Mark Thompson a while back." Fiona raised her eyebrows, waiting for Brigid's reaction.

"You're kidding? Mark? Wasn't he married to MaryAnn?" Brigid gasped.

"Yep, still is. He was seen leaving a bar with Maggie a few times late at night. I don't know much more than that." Fiona waved her hand in the air. "Could be something to it, could be all talk. I don't have a clue."

"Wow, this is a lot to take in, Fiona." Brigid still couldn't quite wrap her head around what she was hearing.

"That's why I'm warning you. It's not that I don't think you can't take care of yourself. You've certainly proved that by now. I just want you to be very aware of what you're getting yourself into, so you don't let your guard down. You're a good person, maybe too trusting, and it seems Maggie has a habit of messing with good people."

The door chime rang, letting them know someone had come into the store. "You can get the bags with the clothes in them out of the back of my car. I hope her daughter can get some use out of them." She smiled and patted her sister on the shoulder.

"Thanks, Fiona." Brigid waved to her as she left the store. If the things Fiona had told her were true, she understood why Maggie had been beating herself up over her past. Maybe if she truly felt remorseful for everything she'd done it would help her stay on the right path. She wanted to help Holly out, but she didn't want to enable Maggie to go back to her old ways.

Sobriety was such a finicky thing. Brigid hoped by donating the clothes to them that Maggie would take it for what Brigid meant it to be, help, not a handout. The last thing Brigid wanted to do was make things worse. She left the bookstore and drove across town to the trailer park where Maggie and Holly lived.

She climbed up the rickety wooden steps of their trailer and knocked on the door, listening for sounds of movement inside. Brigid didn't hear anything, so after a few moments, she knocked again. No one came to the door.

She walked back to her car, wrote a quick note, and deposited the bags in front of the door of the trailer. She put the note on top and picked up a rock from the gravel driveway to hold it down. In the note, she asked them to go through the clothes and pass on anything they didn't want. She said if they needed anything to call her. She left, hoping the clothes would help Holly.

CHAPTER TEN

MaryAnn Thompson ran her fingers through her brunette hair and looked at herself in the mirror. She felt she still looked fairly good for her age. She'd recently had blonde highlights put in to help disguise some of the grey strands that were starting to show up. She pulled it back in a hair tie and sighed. She turned sideways, looking at her profile in the mirror. She was wearing her favorite leggings and a plain grey fitted tee. It was a little cool out this evening, but once she started jogging she knew her body would warm up.

She left the bathroom and stepped into her bedroom. Sitting down on her bed she put on her shoes and laced them, thinking about her day. It all started when she'd been at the grocery store that morning. MaryAnn had run into Beth who she knew from church. They'd been chatting away when Beth had the nerve to ask something MaryAnn thought she had no business to mention.

"MaryAnn, I hate to ask this, but are you and Mark alright?"

At first, MaryAnn had looked at her blankly. *Why wouldn't we be okay?* she'd thought. How terrible it had been to be yanked from that blissful state of forgetting back to the memory of her husband's infidelity. She'd flinched once she remembered, but she tried to brush it off.

"Of course, we are. Why wouldn't we be?" she'd said in a

defensive tone of voice.

"Oh, no reason. I just thought I'd heard otherwise." Beth had started fidgeting.

"Please tell me what you've heard."

Realizing she'd brought this on herself and she should have kept quiet about it, Beth didn't have much choice but to answer MaryAnn. "I heard Mark had been unfaithful with that drunk Maggie Lewis. Someone told me they saw him leaving a bar with her a few times."

Rage had coursed through MaryAnn, burning a path down her spine. She felt sick, but she couldn't let Beth see that what she'd said had so adversely affected her. Instead she'd simply said, "They must have been mistaken."

A moment later, MaryAnn had left, telling Beth she needed to go to the church to meet with Missy. It was true, she did need to meet with Missy about the church fundraiser next month, but mainly she just wanted to get away from Beth. She'd felt like falling apart right there in the grocery store, but she'd blinked back the tears until she was in the safety of her SUV.

She couldn't help it. The tears came, and she'd cried for what felt like the ten millionth time over everything that had happened. She cried for the blow to her marriage, her self-esteem, and the misplaced faith she'd had in her husband. Sometimes she felt as if everyone in Cottonwood Springs knew what had happened, and they were all whispering about it behind her back.

MaryAnn didn't dare admit the truth to anyone. That would mean admitting defeat. She'd been the most popular girl in high school. She'd even been the prom queen. Admitting to anyone that someone like Maggie Lewis could tempt her husband away from her was not possible. Instead, she'd done her best to sweep it all under the rug as if it had never happened.

Thankfully, their son was off at college, and he wouldn't have to hear the rumors or see that his mom and dad didn't sleep in the same room anymore. Even though she and Mark were getting to an age where most people didn't have any more children, they'd decided a few years ago when their son reached the teen years that they wanted another child. After Mark had finally admitted what he'd done, MaryAnn couldn't stand to be near him. He disgusted her. There was no way she'd allow him to touch her after he'd been with Maggie.

When she got to the church, her day went even further downhill. Just as she entered the front of the church, she'd seen Maggie and Missy coming out the door at the far corner. They were talking and laughing, so they didn't notice MaryAnn hurry into the ladies' room near the front door. Watching her friend laugh and enjoy spending time with Maggie hurt her deeply. It was almost as if Maggie was trying to take everyone she loved away from her.

Walking out of her bedroom, MaryAnn headed for the front door. Her phone was already in her armband and her playlist queued up.

"Where are you off to?" Mark asked as she made a beeline to the door. She shoved her earbuds in, pretending she hadn't heard him. Once outside, she began her slow jog around town. *It would have been better if I'd been the one murdered and not poor Lucy,* she thought. *I wouldn't have to see Maggie and wonder what the next thing would be that she was going to take from me.*

The more she thought about it, the more MaryAnn realized she wanted Maggie to die. She had such a burning hatred for the woman, she was almost certain she could do it herself if the opportunity ever presented itself.

*****

Mark watched the door shut behind his wife. She'd always been a pain, but ever since his affair with Maggie, she was even worse. What he couldn't get her to see was that it was this exact attitude of hers that had led him to Maggie in the first place.

He remembered the first night he and Maggie had talked. They'd known each other in school, but he was the rich popular kid, while she was poor with few friends. It would be hard to find two people in more different social circles.

Mark had never realized how kind and funny Maggie could be. After being with MaryAnn for so long, he'd started to feel that all women were domineering and rude. That first night with Maggie was like a cool glass of water after he'd been barely surviving the scorching desert of his marriage to MaryAnn. Maggie was sweet, attentive, caring, and had actually listened to him when he talked. When they'd run into each other a few days later, she'd remembered what he'd said, and that was when he'd started falling for her.

The fall had been fast and hard. When he finally admitted it to her after they'd made love in the back seat of his car, she said she couldn't see him again. She told him she'd found someone she could be with, and she wouldn't have to keep it a secret. Mark had told her he was willing to leave MaryAnn, but that only seemed to push Maggie farther away. He had no clue what he'd done to make her leave, but she had.

He went back to the bar where they'd met as often as he could, hoping to see her again. He'd even sent her flowers at work, but he'd been told she never even took them home. It didn't help that he still had to keep up the pretense of his marriage to MaryAnn. He knew he was one of those men who couldn't be alone, but now everything was so much worse. For the first time he'd experienced what it was like to have a really good relationship with someone you cared about, only to have it ripped from him.

He'd never known he had the ability to love someone so much yet hate them so intensely. He loathed Maggie for making him even more miserable than MaryAnn did, because remembering how he'd felt when he was with her, that amazing chemistry and connection, and then only to have it jerked away… that was cruel. It made him so angry he didn't know if he would hug Maggie or strangle her if she was standing right in front of him.

Mark decided he'd head to the bar one more time to see if she was there. He couldn't stop thinking about her, and it was driving him nuts. If Maggie would just talk to him, he knew he could bring her to her senses. He could easily take care of her financially. Since inheriting his family's business, he was one of the richest men in town.

Maggie wouldn't have to worry about anything if she was with him. All he wanted was to get her everything she wanted, let her get her hair done, and buy nicer clothes. She shouldn't have to work in a factory. He knew she had a shady past, but he was confident they could overcome that.

He took his jacket off the coat rack, slipped it on, and walked outside. *Wait a minute, she lives over in the trailer park,* he thought. *Maybe she'll be out walking to the bar, and I can see her. If nothing else, I can give her a ride, and we'll have a chance to be alone and talk.* He decided that was probably the best way to approach her. He knew rumors had started running around town, and MaryAnn had made sure he knew about them, so he had to keep the risk of being seen to a minimum.

She has to talk to me, he thought as he climbed into his car. *She has to listen. There's no way she doesn't feel the same way I do. Not after some of the things she said.* He put the car in reverse and backed down the driveway, while he continued to think about what he could do to get Maggie back.

She was going to have to give in to him, and he wouldn't take no for an answer this time. He realized that part of her hesitation was because his marriage would break up and cause problems, but as long as he could be with her, it didn't really matter. He no longer cared who saw them together. He didn't want her to be with anyone but him.

CHAPTER ELEVEN

Brigid was sound asleep when her phone began to ring. At first it had entered her dream, where she struggled to find the source of the ringing. She finally jerked herself awake, realizing that her phone really was ringing and wasn't a part of the dream. She threw back the bed covers and reached for it.

"Hello?" Her voice cracked as she struggled to collect her thoughts. She looked over at the clock and saw it was 5:27 in the morning. She couldn't figure out why anyone would be calling her at this early hour unless there was some sort of an emergency.

"Hey, Brigid? It's Sheriff Davis. Sorry if I woke ya', but I could really use yer' help. Ya' know a Maggie and Holly Lewis, don'tcha?"

"I've met them. What's wrong?" Brigid asked as she rubbed her hand across her face, trying to collect herself.

"It'd be better if I told ya' in person. Can ya' come down to Father Jordan's church? I know it's early but…" he let his sentence trail off as he started speaking to someone.

"Of course, just give me a few minutes to get dressed." Brigid ended the call and changed into the jeans she'd worn the previous day and the first shirt she saw in her closet. She didn't know what was going on, but she was certain that Sheriff Davis wouldn't call her this early in the morning unless it was something important.

She grabbed a clean pair of socks and her shoes as she hurried into the great room. Jett was sound asleep on his loveseat. "Good morning, Jett," she said. He yawned and lifted his head, as if he was wondering what was going on.

"Do you need to go out, Jett?" she asked as she rushed into the kitchen. Thankfully, she'd pre-set her automatic coffee pot, so there was already some coffee brewing. She quickly poured herself a cup while Jett dragged himself off his loveseat. She added her favorite creamer to her coffee and stirred it, joining Jett at the back door and letting him out.

Knowing he'd be fine for a little while, she picked up her cell phone and purse, along with her keys, and headed out the front door. When she was in her car, she sent a text to Linc.

Sheriff Davis just called me and asked me to come to the Jordan's church. When you wake up would you go over to my house and see if Jett wants back in the house and then feed him? You know where the emergency key is. I'll let you know what's going on when I learn more.

She pushed send and dropped the phone onto the passenger seat. As she started her car and prepared to back out of the driveway the phone lit up, indicating she had a message.

That's strange. Not a problem. I'll check on Jett in 20 - 30 minutes. Want me to hang out with him until you get back? I don't have anything to do this morning that can't wait.

Brigid smiled at her phone. She was glad she and Linc had told each other where they kept their emergency keys. At times like this it was handy.

That would be perfect. I don't think you could get out of the house without him following you. Thank you.

She put the phone back down and backed out of the driveway. As she navigated through town she began to wonder what the issue was with Maggie and Holly. *I hope Maggie hasn't relapsed and done something foolish,* she thought. She'd been so hopeful that Maggie could get her life in order. She really didn't want her to slide back into her old habits. That would be so hard on Holly.

After meeting Holly a few days earlier, she could tell she didn't completely believe that her mother would stay sober. Brigid understood why she felt that way. She couldn't imagine what it must be like to live with a mother who placed substance abuse ahead of her daughter's welfare. That had to create emotional scars that couldn't be easily healed.

As Brigid turned onto the road where the church was located, she saw a number of law enforcement cars and yellow tape. The terrible memories of Lucy's murder flashed before her. The sheriff's cars, with their flashing red and blue lights, brought back things she'd rather forget. She pulled into the church parking lot, turned off the engine, and got out of her car.

"Oh, Brigid," she heard a familiar voice say. Missy broke free from a group of people who were standing outside the main doors of the church. Her face was pale and streaked with tears. Her nose and eyes were red, and she had a wad of tissues clutched in her hand. She was still wearing a bathrobe and slippers. When she reached Brigid, she wrapped her arms around her friend and began to sob.

"Glad yer' here," Sheriff Davis said. He'd also left the group of people and joined Brigid and Missy.

"What's going on?" Brigid asked, confused, as Missy clung to her.

"Maggie Lewis was murdered," Davis said softly. "Seems someone strangled her while she was in the chapel area. Probably doin' a bit of soul searchin' or prayin'."

"Oh no," Brigid gasped, her hand flying up to cover her mouth. "In the church?"

Sheriff Davis nodded grimly. "I know, jes' ain't right. One of my deputies is talkin' to her daughter right now. Says she knows ya'."

Brigid was shocked that the girl would mention her, but then she remembered Maggie and Holly had told her they had no family living nearby. Was it possible she was the only one Holly would think to call? Brigid nodded, acknowledging to the sheriff that she knew Holly. Her mouth was dry, and her throat felt tight.

"Know yer' a busy woman and all, so I hate to ask this of ya' but I may need a coupla' favors." Davis' brow was bunched with worry.

"What can I do?" Brigid managed to squeak out. Her voice cracked, and she felt overwhelmed. She was still trying to understand why he'd called her.

"Had one of my deputies go to Maggie's home to wake Holly up and tell her about her mother. Didn't want her to find out about it on the mornin' news program. The preacher's wife went with my deputy to help out. They brought her back here to the church, and I've got her sittin' over there on the church steps with one of my female deputies who's tryin' to comfort her.

"I unnerstand ya' knew Maggie and Holly and were trying' to help 'em out. Now, that Maggie's gone, Holly's next of kin is in Missouri. Some aunt the kid's never met. She really don't wanna' leave Cottonwood Springs and she told me she'd like to stay with you, so I thought I'd see if you'd be willin' to let her stay at your place? It's fine if ya' don't want to..."

Brigid cut him off. "That's perfectly fine. If she'd like to, she's welcome to stay with me." Brigid couldn't fathom making the girl have to move that far away to live with people she didn't even know. Although Brigid barely knew her, at least she'd be able to finish the school year here in Cottonwood Springs.

"That's great, Brigid. Thanks. Already tol' her ya' might be willin' to let her stay with ya' fer a while. Think she'll appreciate it, too. She's been worried sick. Poor thing."

He sighed and looked toward the young girl. She was sitting on the steps of the church, her face red and blotchy, wearing a pair of plaid pajama pants that had been in one of the sacks of clothes Brigid had given her, and a faded black shirt. Her hair was a mess, and she was barefoot. Brigid's heart filled with sadness as she looked at the forlorn young girl. In one swift terrible moment, whoever had done this to her mother had taken away the only family Holly had ever known.

"The other thing I wanted to ask ya' was if you'd mind helpin' me with this investigation. Ya' know, like the last one we did together? Realize it ain't yer' job, but ya' was so good at getting' people to open up when Lucy was murdered. Think you got a nose for this kinda' thing," Sheriff Davis said as he looked at her anxiously.

For a moment Brigid was tempted to tell him no. She remembered what it had been like helping him with the investigation of her friend Lucy's murder, and she wasn't sure if she was willing to take on that responsibility again. Then her mind replayed the conversation she'd had with Maggie, when she admitted how she wanted to right her wrongs and develop a real relationship with her daughter. Whoever did this had robbed Maggie of her chance to do that and prove to the world she was more than just an addict. Just thinking about it made Brigid's heart ache.

Brigid looked over at Holly. She was nodding and talking to the female deputy. Even though she was stony-faced, Brigid could see the pain in her eyes. How could Brigid refuse to help find the killer and thereby possibly deny the young woman the comfort of knowing that whoever took her mother from her was behind bars?

"Okay, I'll help," Brigid finally said. The words left her mouth before she'd consciously made the decision to say them, but once they were out she knew she'd done the right thing.

"Good," Sheriff Davis said. "When my deputies are done with her ya' can take her to her home and let her collect some clothes and personal items. We've asked her to leave everythin' jes' as it is in case there's some clue as to who the killer is. Once we've had a chance to thoroughly search the trailer, she'll be able to return and take whatever else she needs." Sheriff Davis touched Brigid's arm. "Yer' a good person for doin' this, Brigid. I know it ain't easy, and I realize I'm askin' a mighty lot from you."

"Don't mention it," Brigid said touching his hand before he moved away to join the other officers.

"That poor girl," Missy said tearfully as she stood next to Brigid. Brigid had forgotten her friend was standing beside her.

"I know. I can't imagine what she's going through right now," Brigid said with a sigh, "Before I talk to her, I probably ought to know what happened. Want to tell me?"

Missy wiped her eyes before she started to speak. "I'd just gotten out of bed, and Jordan said he was going to make his morning rounds. He likes to check the grounds, the chapel area, and so on in the morning, just to make sure everything's as it should be. When he walked in the chapel through one of the side doors that leads to the back of the church, he didn't notice anything at first.

"Maggie was up closer to the front, so the pews blocked her from his view. It wasn't until he circled around and started heading back that he noticed her laying on the floor. He ran over to her, thinking maybe she was unconscious, but when he got closer he saw the bruising on her throat and her eyes staring vacantly at the ceiling. He hurriedly called 911, and then he called me."

Missy's eyes began to tear up again. "I'm starting to think I'm cursed," she said with a sob.

"Why in the world would you think that?" Brigid asked, stroking her friend's back.

"First it was Lucy, and now it's Maggie. Both of them were my friends, and now they're gone." Tears ran down Missy's cheeks.

"Missy," Brigid said, pulling her friend close. "None of this is your fault. They'll find out who did it and why, just like with Lucy. None of this is because of you. You'll see."

Brigid continued to comfort her and then she saw the officer who had been talking to Holly walk away from the child. "Missy, I have to go help Holly now. Are you going to be alright?"

"Yeah, I think so. We'll have to move the church service outside this morning. I just can't imagine anyone murdering someone in a church," Missy said as she dabbed her eyes.

"Me neither, but right now I need to see about getting Holly settled in at my house. Let me know if you need anything," Brigid said.

She left her friend and approached the young girl. The two times Brigid had seen her before, she'd had the impression that the girl was older than her age, but now she looked like a broken waif.

"I'm so sorry, Holly," Brigid said and opened her arms. Holly quickly stepped into them and allowed Brigid to wordlessly comfort her.

"Who could have done this to her?" she asked, her voice muffled by Brigid's shirt.

"I don't know, honey, but they'll find out who did it." She gently squeezed Holly before letting her go. "Are you sure you want to stay with me?" she asked.

Holly nodded. "If it's all right with you. Besides Missy, you're the only one who has ever helped me. I don't want to move to Missouri. I've never even met my aunt. Maybe later on, but not right now."

"I understand," Brigid said. "You don't need to make any decisions yet, Holly. Let's get you a few things from your trailer, and then I'll take you back to my place, so you can get settled in. There's no rush."

"The sheriff told me I can only take clothes and the stuff I need for school," Holly said forlornly, as Brigid led her to her car.

"I know. They told me the same thing, but they just want to make sure they don't miss any clues that might be in the trailer and could be used to lead them to your mother's killer."

"I know, but it still sucks," Holly said as she got into Brigid's car.

"Yeah, it does," Brigid said.

CHAPTER TWELVE

Brigid pushed the front door of her home open and helped Holly carry the trash bag full of her belongings over the threshold. Jett hopped up from where he'd been laying on the floor beside Linc's feet.

"Holly, this is Jett," she said introducing her to the big dog. She bent down and scratched him behind the ears before looking up at Linc, "And this is Linc Olson. He's my next-door neighbor. We've been seeing each other for a little while now. Guys, this is Holly Lewis. She's going to be staying here for a while."

Linc stood up and shook Holly's hand. "Nice to meet you, Holly." Linc smiled, not looking the least bit ruffled by what was happening. Brigid smiled at him encouragingly and sent him a look of gratitude.

"I'll show you your room, Holly, and you can get settled in there." Brigid led Holly down the hall, Jett right behind them. "Here you are," she said as she pushed open the door. "The bathroom is at the end of the hall. I have one attached to my room, so you can consider that one yours. My bedroom's the next one down the hall, and my office is across from it. Feel free to rearrange and put things anywhere you'd like in here."

Holly nodded. Her eyes began to tear up again. "Thank you, Brigid. I can't tell you how grateful I am that you're letting me stay with you. When they told me about mom…" Holly broke off into a sob. Brigid pulled her close and let her cry for a few minutes.

"Holly, don't worry about it. You can stay here as long as you like. I'll have a few ground rules, but I don't think they'll be a problem. We'll talk about them later." She gently patted Holly's shoulder.

Jett bumped into Holly's leg and whined to get her attention. Holly smiled at him and squatted down to his level. "You're a sweetie, aren't you?" she said through her tears as she scratched his head. She looked up at Brigid, "I think I'm going to lay down for a little bit and rest, if that's okay with you?"

"Of course. Would you like me to take Jett?" Brigid asked.

Holly looked down at the dog and shook her head from side to side.

"Okay, just make sure you leave the door open a little, so he can get out if he wants. Otherwise he might break down the door." Both of them laughed at that mental image. Brigid walked over to the door and turned back towards Holly, "Do you have any foods you really don't like?" she asked.

"No, I pretty much eat everything, I even eat Brussels sprouts," Holly said.

"Okay, rest for as long as you need to. Let me know if you get hungry." Brigid slipped into the hall, pulling the door partially closed behind her. When she returned to the front room, Linc was sitting on the couch, waiting for her. His eyebrows were raised in a silent question.

"Let's talk outside," she whispered when she drew closer. Linc stood up and followed her to the back door, where they quietly went outside and sat at the table and chairs on the porch. Brigid raised the maroon umbrella, so they could have some shade from the bright early morning sun.

"What happened?" Linc asked.

"Remember how I told you I was cleaning out my closet to help a young girl whose mother I'd met at the church?" she asked. Linc nodded. "Well that was Holly. Her mother was murdered this morning. Father Jordan found her body in the chapel at the church. The only relative Holly has is an aunt in Missouri she's never even met, so she asked the sheriff if she could stay with me. I didn't know what else to do but say yes," Brigid said with a sigh.

"That poor girl," Linc said. "I can't imagine."

"I know. She pretty much just got her mother back from her addictions, and now someone's taken her away again. This time permanently." She shook her head. "I figure she can stay with me until she's finished out this school year. She may end up changing her mind and want to go live with her aunt. I don't know, but I couldn't make her move away from the only place she's ever known, not right after losing her mother. She's resting now."

"I admire you for doing that," Linc said as he reached across the table for her hand. She took it and smiled. They heard a car approaching Brigid's house. "I think you have a visitor," Linc said. They stood up and walked around to the front of the house, so they wouldn't disturb Holly.

When they rounded the corner, they saw Sheriff Davis climbing out of his car. "Brigid, Linc," he said touching the brim of his hat. "How's Holly doin'?"

"She's resting right now," Brigid said. "Jett's keeping her company."

"Good. She needs it. Gotta' moment to talk?" Davis asked.

"We were sitting out back to give Holly a little quiet time. Okay if we talk there?" Brigid asked.

"Lead the way," the sheriff said.

The three of them sat down at the table on the porch. The day was starting to warm up, and the dew was quickly evaporating off of the grass. Each of them was very careful to be quiet as they sat down in their chairs, even though Holly probably wouldn't have heard them.

"Thanks for lettin' her stay here, Brigid. Know it ain't what I'm supposed to do, but I just couldn't bear to put such a good kid in the Child Protective Services system. I feel like I've practically watched her grow up. We've had to check on her a few times more than I'd like to count when her mother wasn't doin' so hot. I don't think the kid'll give ya' any trouble." Davis slid his jacket off and hung it on the back of the chair. "If ya' change yer' mind, lemme' know."

"I will," Brigid said. "So, exactly what happened to Maggie? I didn't get any details from Missy. She was having trouble coping with Maggie's murder, and as close as she and Maggie were, I can't blame her."

"Looks like someone strangled her with one of them curtain tieback ropes used in the church. Ya' know, them gold ones. Father Jordan noticed it was missin', so we done some preliminary testin' with one of the other ones, and it seems to be a match for the marks on her neck." Sheriff Davis subconsciously rubbed his neck, as though he could feel something wrapped around it.

"I tried talkin' to Missy earlier about anyone she thought might be capable of doin' this. She tried to think of someone, but she was too upset. Everythin' was just a little overwhelmin' for her considerin'…" He let his sentence trail off. Brigid and Linc nodded in agreement. They knew he was referring to when Brigid and Missy had found their friend Lucy lying murdered on the kitchen floor of her B & B.

"I can talk to her later, if you'd like," Brigid offered.

"That'd be great," Sheriff Davis said. "I don't want to upset her any more than she already is. Need to get a list of suspects together as soon as possible. I know you're aware of how 'portant it is we get the ball rollin'. Time is of the essence here."

Brigid nodded. "I know Missy and Maggie talked a lot about her past. Maggie had brought up doing bad things in her former life that she wanted to make up for. I would think whoever those people are could possibly be suspects."

Sheriff Davis nodded. "If ya' could get a list of suspects together, that'd be great. We'll keep workin' on our end, but if you can work yer' magic like ya' done last time, ya' can really help me out." The dispatcher's voice came through on his radio, interrupting their conversation. When he was finished answering he turned his radio down.

"Also, if ya' can, I'd appreciate if you'd ask Holly if she can think of anyone that mighta' been upset with her mother lately. Know I'm askin' a lot, but people tend to clam up when they see the uniform." He shrugged. "Can't say as I blame 'em, but we need answers soon as we can get 'em."

"Will do," Brigid nodded. "I'll talk to them both today." She looked toward the house, thinking, before turning back to Sheriff Davis. "What about school? I know she does well and gets good grades, but I can't imagine that she'll want to go back right away after this. Is there any way she can have her school work sent here? It would give her something to do and keep her mind busy on other things."

"That's a good idea," Linc said.

"I'll get ahold of John Bartlett. He's the principal. I'm sure he can work somethin' out. I know tomorrow's Monday but let her know I'll take care of it. I'll call ya' when I know more," he said. He began to tap his chin, "I know there was somethin' else I was needin' to tell ya'…" He was quiet for a moment, then he said, "Oh yeah. Right before I got out of the car, one of my deputies let me know they're done over at the trailer. Whenever Holly feels up to it, she can take whatever she wants outta' it. If ya' need any help movin' things, let me know."

"We can use my truck, if you'd like," Linc offered. "I can help carry the heavier stuff."

"Ya' need any more manpower, ya' just give me a holler. Me or one of the deputies will come help. Jes' say the word." With that, Sheriff Davis stood up and stretched. "The day started out purty early fer me, and I got a feelin' it ain't gonna' end anytime soon. Lemme' know what ya' find out, and Linc, keep an eye on her," he said pointing to Brigid.

"You know I will, Sheriff," Linc said, winking at her. Brigid rolled her eyes and smiled.

"Call me later when ya' get a list together, so we can get started." He stood up, threw his jacket over his shoulder, touched his hand to the brim of his hat, and walked around the corner of the house towards his car.

"You want me to tag along with you today?" Linc asked after the sheriff left.

"No, that's okay," Brigid said. "I know you had plans. Besides, I don't see myself getting into too much trouble visiting Missy."

"If you change your mind, just let me know." He looked at the time on his phone and sighed. "I better get to it. Between some chores I have to do around the house and wrapping up a bit of client work, I do have a full day ahead of me." He stood and leaned over Brigid. He cupped her chin before kissing her gently. "Once Holly gets settled we should have dinner together."

"That's a great idea," Brigid said. "Tonight, I think it would be better if it was just Holly and me, so we can get to know each other a little more. You don't mind, do you?"

"Of course not," Linc said. He yawned. "I think there may be a nap in my future."

Brigid couldn't help but yawn, too. "I think you're right." She stood and gave him another kiss and pulled him close. Brigid felt a bit unnerved, but she didn't want to let Linc know that. It wasn't as though she felt she was in any danger. Far from it. It was just the thought that once again there was someone out there who had murdered another human being in cold blood in the small town of Cottonwood Springs. Her heart ached for the young woman who was now under her care.

She waved to Linc as she watched him disappear around the corner of the house. When he was gone, she slipped back inside, quietly shutting the door behind her. Creeping through the house, she tiptoed down the hall until she was outside what was now Holly's room. She'd been thinking about redecorating the room, and evidently someone had been listening. Now it would be Holly's. Sometime soon she'd take Holly to buy paint and allow her to paint the bedroom whatever color she wished. The existing beiged color walls had never been one of Brigid's favorites.

Gently pushing the door open, Brigid peeked around the corner. Jett was curled up on the bed with Holly, both of them napping. She had her arm draped over him. Jett opened his eyes and looked at Brigid, but he didn't move. She had a feeling he was there more for support than anything. She was learning that Jett was an extremely empathetic dog with a huge heart. He closed his eyes again, and Brigid silently backed out of the room.

Still being quiet, she walked to her bedroom, yawning once again. Considering how early she'd gotten up, she decided a short nap wouldn't hurt. She set her alarm to wake her up in an hour and snuggled down under the covers. It didn't take long until everyone in the house was fast asleep.

CHAPTER THIRTEEN

Before she sat down at the kitchen table, Brigid slid two plates, each with a turkey sandwich and chips on them across the table. One for her and one for Holly.

"How are you feeling?" Brigid asked after she was seated at the table.

"Like everything is a dream. It seems surreal." Holly picked her sandwich up and took a bite, but she seemed distracted.

"What's wrong?" Brigid asked. She could tell the girl was bothered by something and wasn't talking about it. She didn't want to pry, but she also wanted Holly to know she was there for support if she needed it.

"I don't know," Holly began. "It's hard to put into words. I don't want…" She stopped suddenly.

"Don't want what?" Brigid prodded.

"I don't want you to think I'm a bad person." Holly's eyes met Brigid's.

"Why would I think that? You can talk to me, Holly. I promise I'm not going to judge you. I'm sure you have a ton of things swirling around in your mind, and that's perfectly normal," Brigid said as she took a bite of her sandwich.

"Is it bad that I'm kind of relieved she's gone? I mean, I loved her but…" She let the sentence trail off.

"But she was a handful?" Brigid suggested.

"Yeah, kind of. I was so used to the mom who would disappear and leave me to take care of myself. It feels like she's just on one of her benders, you know? Like she's just off doing her own thing again and abandoned me in the process."

"I think it's perfectly understandable for you to feel that way, Holly. Don't be too harsh on yourself. You're probably going to have all sorts of emotions in the next few weeks, and it's healthy to talk about them."

Brigid stopped and looked at Holly, debating whether or not it was the right time to ask Holly if she had any idea who could have killed her mother. She decided this was as good a time as any. "I hate to ask you this, Holly, but Sheriff Davis wondered if you had any thoughts on who could have done this to your mother?"

Holly's eyes flashed and met Brigid's. "I've been thinking about that a lot," she began. "I know Mom screwed over a lot of people, but I don't know exactly who. I suppose it could be any one of them, but I kind of don't think it was."

"Why?" Brigid asked. Jett joined the two of them at the kitchen table and flopped down between their feet, hoping they might drop something on the floor.

Holly pulled the crust off her bread and fed it to him. "I don't know, a hunch maybe? I think either Billy or Sam probably knows something."

"Billy or Sam? Who are they?" Brigid asked.

"Billy is, well, he was Mom's boyfriend. She broke up with him when he wouldn't get sober with her. He's been hounding her ever since. She was ignoring his calls, texts, and even tried to avoid him when she saw him at the store. He was getting pretty persistent, though." Holly shook her head. "He's a real piece of…" She caught herself before swearing. "Work," she said, finishing the sentence. "Sam was one of Mom's druggie friends. Neither one of them ever paid any attention to me, but I saw the way Sam looked at Billy and my mom. She was jealous of my mother."

"Really? Like she wanted Billy?" Brigid asked.

"Exactly. I don't know why, but I feel like they know something." Holly started to chew on her fingernail.

"Well, if they do, I'm sure the police will find out. Do you know what their last names are? I'll be talking to Sheriff Davis later, and I can tell him about them, if that's all right with you."

"Sure. Their names are Billy Watkins and Samantha Rogers. I'm sure he'll know who they are."

Brigid stood up and took her empty plate to the sink. "I have a few things I need to do. You're welcome to tag along with me if you'd like to, or you can stay here and watch TV or get on the internet." She leaned back against the sink for a moment while she waited for Holly to respond.

"What kind of cable do you have?" Holly asked.

"I have the big package. Just scroll through if you want. There's also Hulu and Netflix. Feel free to make your own profiles. There's a computer in my office if you'd like to get online." She took a deep breath and then she continued, "Holly, I know you're a smart girl, and you've been taking care of yourself for a long time, but I'd really appreciate it if you didn't go into town alone for a while.

"Let's face it. There's a killer out there. Jett's been trained, so he'll protect you here at the house. He'll let you know if he needs to go out, but he shouldn't need to for a while. There's plenty of food in the fridge, and when you'd like to, we can go the store and get some of your favorite foods."

Holly nodded. "I don't really have anywhere I want to go. I'd kind of like to lay low, so I think I'll stay here if that's okay with you. I promise I won't get into trouble."

"That's fine. I'll leave my cell phone number tacked on the fridge, and Linc's number too. He's my friend and next door neighbor. If there's an emergency, don't hesitate to call him. He'll be over in no time."

A little later Brigid pulled up in front of Missy and Jordan's home which was located behind the church. She'd called Missy to make sure she was home and to see if she wanted a little company. When she got out of her car, she saw Missy sitting on the porch in a wicker rocking chair. The large home was painted white and accented with deep blue shutters on either side of the large front windows. Pillows in the same color of blue were on the wicker porch furniture. A wrap-around screened-in porch was attached to the house. The effect was one of an elegant old farmhouse.

When Missy saw Brigid, she stood up and walked over to the screen door, holding it open for her. When she was inside the porch, Brigid hugged her. "How are you doing, Missy?" she asked.

"Slightly better now. I'm sorry for the way I acted this morning." She sat back down on the rocker while Brigid sat in one of the wicker chairs. "Would you like some lemonade?" Missy asked. She had a pitcher and an extra glass sitting on the low table in front of her.

"Sure, thank you." Brigid said.

"How's Holly holding up?" Missy asked as she poured the lemonade. "I've been thinking of that poor girl all morning."

"She's okay. She's at home right now, resting. We still have to get the rest of her stuff from Maggie's trailer, so she can fully settle in. I think I'm going to look for an inexpensive laptop for her. That way, she'll be able to get online while I work."

"Brigid, I have one she can have. We recently upgraded the laptop I use, and there's not a thing wrong with it. I just decided to get a newer one, because it was on sale. Mine's only about two years old. Remind me before you leave, and I'll get it for you." Missy smiled. "That would make me feel good. I've been trying to figure out what I was going to do with it, and also what I could do for Holly."

"Thanks Missy. I'm sure she'll be excited about it."

"Tell her I'll stop by and visit her in a few days. I'd do it sooner, but I just…" Missy couldn't finish her sentence. She was too choked up and fighting back tears.

"Don't worry about it. You need to take care of yourself, too. You and Maggie seemed to be very close," Brigid said. "I know this has to be very hard on you."

She nodded. "It is. I just don't understand how this could happen." Missy sniffed. "I mean, who would murder someone in a church?"

"I don't know. I'm helping Sheriff Davis collect leads now," Brigid said. "Do you have any idea of who might have done it?"

"You bet I do." Missy said with conviction. "As a matter of fact, I have several thoughts on who might have done it. I began thinking about it when I came back to the house and started to clean. I think best when I'm cleaning, you know," she said as a side note.

"Who did you come up with?" Brigid asked as she pulled a small notebook out of her purse, so she could take notes.

"First off, there's Frank Sterling. He was very vocal in his hatred of Maggie."

"Really? Why?" Brigid decided not to tell Missy that she'd already heard something about Frank from Fiona.

"His father used to live on his own, and he had some sort of disability service that paid people to come in and do things for him around the house. He could pick the person who was hired, but the company paid them. Maggie was working for the company, and they sent her to his house. As I understand it, she did a great job for a while. She was pretty strung out back then, though. She admitted to me she'd convinced Paul, Frank's father, that things should be put away in the attic for safekeeping. Instead, she'd steal them, so she could trade or sell them for drugs or alcohol."

"Wow." Brigid's eyes opened wide, pretending to be shocked.

"Yeah. Maggie wasn't proud of what she'd done. When she needed money, she'd tell Paul that the company wasn't paying her on time. She'd ask him for a loan and promise to deposit the money into his account when she got paid."

"Only she never did," Brigid concluded, thinking this was exactly what Fiona had told her the day before.

"Exactly. She ended up draining his bank account. Paul went downhill fairly fast after he found out what had happened. I understand he was depressed and hurt. Frank moved his father in with him not long after that." Missy took a sip of her lemonade and waited to see what Brigid had to say.

"I can see why he was mad, but I'm not sure that's cause for murder," Brigid said.

"I'd agree with you, but that was before Frank went off on Maggie right here at the church. He came in one Sunday and saw her sitting in a pew before the service. He made a big scene when he saw her. Said he wouldn't go to any church she attended, and she deserved to rot and burn in Hell for all eternity for what she'd done.

"This happened when she'd first gotten clean. I was trying to calm him down when Maggie rushed out of church. After that, she'd wait until the service had started and slip in the back and then leave before it was over to avoid him."

"You're saying just the sight of her set him off. Right?" Brigid knew who Frank Sterling was, and he wasn't known for being a calm, cool-headed man, even in the best of times.

"Definitely."

"Anyone else?" Brigid asked.

"Maggie did mention that her ex-boyfriend, Billy, had been harassing her lately. She told me he'd corner her when he saw her in a store and try to get her to go places with him. I know she was afraid of him."

"Holly mentioned him this morning along with another friend named Sam," Brigid said, flipping back to the page in her notebook where she'd jotted down the names Holly had given her earlier. "Do you know anything about her?"

Missy shook her head. "Maggie never mentioned her to me." She pursed her lips as she thought. "I know I'm forgetting someone else…. I remember now. It's the Thompsons!"

"Do you mean Mark and MaryAnn Thompson?" Brigid asked. She deliberately tried to look amazed, because she didn't want Missy to know that Fiona had already told her about them.

"Yes, apparently Maggie got tangled up with them as well." Missy paused as Brigid wrote their names down. "I've pieced a few things together from what Maggie told me and from what I've overheard. Unfortunately, some of the women in our congregation are serious gossips. I try to avoid them, but I keep an ear open to see what's going on. It's my understanding that before Maggie was with Billy, Maggie and Mark were having an affair."

"Now, that is unexpected," Brigid said. She knew Mark from school. Growing up, he was always one of the rich kids, and now he was quite wealthy in his own right. His wife, MaryAnn, had been in school with them, too. She'd always been one of the most popular girls in school and was used to getting whatever she wanted. No one was surprised when they got married. It seemed like a match made in heaven.

"To be honest, I was fairly shocked when I heard about it. I guess they met at a local bar and hit it off. They began having an affair and as time went by, things got fairly hot and heavy. Mark got very serious about their relationship and started telling Maggie that he wanted to leave MaryAnn. He said he'd never felt about anyone like he did about Maggie. It freaked Maggie out. She broke things off with him just as the rumors really started to fly.

"Mark became physically violent with Maggie in the parking lot outside the bar after she told him it was over between them. She had bruises on her where he'd grabbed her." Missy shook her head, remembering how dark the bruises were and how Maggie had tried to dismiss the severity of them.

"So, she told you he was fairly aggressive with her. That's not a good sign," Brigid said, writing in her notebook.

"No, it isn't, but you also need to know about MaryAnn."

"Why her?" Brigid asked.

"Once the rumors started about Mark and Maggie, MaryAnn was pretty embarrassed. The town gossip didn't like having things turned around on her. One day I overheard her talking to one of her friends. She swore she was so angry she could kill Maggie for sleeping with her husband and ruining her reputation," Missy said as she sadly shook her head.

"Do you think she meant it?"

"From the way she sounded when she said it, yes. I sure wouldn't want anyone to talk about me that way. She sounded truly evil."

CHAPTER FOURTEEN

Before heading home, Brigid decided to stop and update Sheriff Davis on what she'd found out. If time was of the essence, she didn't want to wait and give the killer a better chance to avoid being captured. She pulled into a parking space in front of the sheriff's office, picked up her purse, and went inside.

"Hi, Brigid. Come on back," Sheriff Davis said as he waved, motioning for her to come into his office. He held the door open for her, and then gently clicked it shut before sitting down at his desk. "Found out anythin'?" He took a yellow notepad out from under a stack of papers, ready to take notes.

"I think so. I definitely have a list of people to start with." Brigid took her notebook out of her purse and said, "First we have the boyfriend, Billy Watkins."

"I know him," the sheriff said. "He's a shady character. Word is he's replaced Mike Loomis as the local go-to drug dealer."

"Evidently Maggie dumped him when he wouldn't get clean with her. According to a couple of people I talked to, he still wanted to have a serious relationship with her, and he's been borderline stalking her since she broke up with him," Brigid said.

"That confirms what we found on her phone. Lots of unopened

texts from him and unanswered calls. He's got a few offenses under his belt. Already have my deputies tryin' to locate him." He nodded. "Who else ya' got?"

"Next is a friend of Maggie's by the name of Samantha Rogers. Holly told me that she thinks the woman was jealous of the relationship between Maggie and Billy and wanted Billy for herself."

Davis nodded. "Ain't much, but sometimes people kill for less. Keep goin'." He picked up a small red ball and began to toss it in the air as he listened.

"The next one is Frank Sterling," Brigid continued. "I understand he's been pretty vocal about his hatred for Maggie ever since she swindled his father out of most of his money."

"I heard about that. Definitely need to find out where he was when the murder was committed." He continued to toss the ball.

"The last two people on my list are MaryAnn and Mark Thompson."

The sheriff stopped tossing the ball when she said their names, looked closely at her, and said in surprise, "Both of 'em?"

Brigid nodded. "It seems that Maggie had an affair with Mark before she started seeing Billy. Mark was very involved with her, and she became afraid of him after she ended it. He even got a little physical with her outside the bar they were at when she ended things."

Davis leaned over his notepad and made some notes. "I hadn't heard that part. Good job, Brigid, but why MaryAnn? Because of the affair?"

"Yes. I talked to someone who overheard her saying she could kill Maggie for what she'd done, disgracing her like that." Brigid shrugged. "Like you said, people have killed for less."

Davis let out a low whistle. "Nice job, Brigid. This gives us somewhere to start. I'm buried in paperwork, but if ya' could check on Frank and the Thompsons, that'd be great. Need to know where everyone was around midnight on Friday. That's the time the preliminary coroner's report lists as the time of murder. Frank'll probably be at work durin' the day, but ya' should be able to talk to his wife. The Thompsons..." He paused to think.

"They still own that furniture store, right?" Brigid supplied.

"Yeah. Haven't heard of 'em hirin' on any help, so he should be there. My deputies ain't had no luck catchin' up with Billy so far. Thought maybe you and I could go over there in plain clothes and see if he'd answer the door. He wouldn't be the first guy that don't open doors when there's a uniform on the other side."

Brigid nodded. "Sure, I can do that. Just give me a call tomorrow when you're ready to go pay him a visit."

"Great," Sheriff Davis stood up from his desk, indicating their meeting was over. "Thanks, Brigid. It's jes' like I thought. Ya' know how to talk to people and get information."

"I'm happy to help, Corey." Brigid stood up and walked towards the door. She paused for a moment, her hand on the knob. "I know Maggie did some terrible things, but I still feel as though deep down inside she was a good person."

"Sometimes good people do bad things, Brigid. If this job has taught me anythin', it's that you jes' never really know what a person's capable of doin'." He sighed. "Take care, now."

*****

"Thanks for driving us, Linc," Brigid said. Linc, Holly and Brigid were on their way to Holly's trailer, so she could get what she wanted from the trailer.

"Yes, thank you," Holly said from her place in the backseat of

Linc's extended cab truck. "I really appreciate it."

Linc smiled at Holly through the rearview mirror. "It's not a problem. I'm happy to help."

As they pulled up outside the old trailer, Holly was overcome with a strange eerie feeling. It was as though two parts of her mind were at odds with each other. Part of her knew and understood that her mother was gone and was not coming back. Yet the other part almost convinced her that Maggie would open the door at any moment and tell her to hurry up and get inside, because dinner was almost ready.

Holly had just started getting used to this new mom, the mother who would ask where she was going and when she'd be back. It was nice to have a warm meal made by someone else instead of having to fend for herself. And her mom could cook. That was one of the things she did extremely well, when she did it.

"Brigid, Linc," Holly said as Linc turned off the truck's engine. "If you don't mind, I'd kind of like a few minutes by myself in there." She didn't know why, but she felt as though she needed to be alone in the trailer.

"Sure," Brigid said. "We'll sit here until you let us know you're ready for us to come in."

"Take your time, Holly. We're not going anywhere," Linc said.

She climbed out of the truck, shutting the door behind her. The gravel beneath the thin soles of her shoes poked at her feet, but she was used to it. It felt like she was home. As she got closer to the trailer, the memory of her last morning at the trailer flooded back. It was all bits and pieces until she pushed open the door and stepped inside.

As she shut the door behind her, she remembered everything that had happened. She'd gotten out of bed before the sun had even come up. She didn't remember exactly what time it had been, but it was that time when it seems like it's still the middle of the night, but it's also early morning. Holly had tried to go back to sleep, but it had been useless. Finally, she'd stumbled out of bed and had gone to the bathroom when she noticed that the light was on in the kitchen. She went down the narrow hall to the tiny kitchen area, expecting to see her mother at the stove or sitting at the little table. When she didn't see her there, she looked in the living room, but Maggie wasn't there either.

She'd looked back towards the kitchen and noticed her mom had left her cell phone on the counter. She'd gone into the kitchen, opened the cabinet, and taken out some pancake mix. She was pretty sure her mother had fallen off the wagon and was out getting drunk or high, although she hated herself for assuming that now.

Why did I have to assume the worst? she chided herself. *Maybe she wouldn't have left the trailer if she thought I'd be more supportive. Maybe, rather than going down the street to the church to pray, she would have woken me up to talk. If she had, she'd still be alive right now.*

Tears began to trickle down Holly's cheeks. The sad thing was, she knew things were better in the few short hours since her mother had been murdered, than they'd ever been when her mother was alive. She hated to admit it, but it was true. She didn't know how long Brigid would let her stay with her, but for now she lived in a nice house, had cable and internet, and even a nice laptop of her own. Plus, she had people around her who didn't seem to have problems with alcohol or drugs. All of those things hadn't been possible when her mother was alive.

She pushed her unpleasant thoughts away and began looking around the living room. She could tell things had been moved when the officers had searched the trailer, but even so, it was pretty much the same as before. She wandered around the room, looking at the worn furniture and the old TV. She picked up the blanket her mother had crocheted that was always draped across the back of the couch. Holding it up to her face, she inhaled the scent deeply. It still smelled like her mom's perfume. A hard lump formed in Holly's throat before she folded it over and started to assemble a pile of things she wanted to take with her.

She looked at the pictures hanging on the wall and pulled down an old photo of her mother, her aunt, and her grandmother. Her mom had been about sixteen when the picture was taken. Holly had never had a chance to meet her grandmother or her aunt. Her grandmother had died shortly after the picture was taken, and her mother had told her that her aunt had moved away a few months later.

Holly put the photo on top of the blanket before she took down another photo. It was one Holly had saved up her money to buy. She and her mother had their picture taken together, and Holly had it blown up. She'd gone to a flea market and spent the rest of her money on a frame. She'd given it to her mother five years ago.

As she looked at the picture, Holly was overwhelmed by a sea of memories of her mom. The lump in her throat returned as she fought to control her emotions. Finally, she succumbed to them and the tears that had been a slow trickle became a river. A sob built up in her chest and broke through all her defenses. A tidal wave of emotions flooded over her as she gripped the photo of her and her mother. She clutched it to her chest, willing herself to go back to that time. She would give anything to go back there, if only for a moment, just to feel her mother's skin, to hear her voice, anything.

Holly sat on the floor and cried for what felt like forever, yet when she looked at the time it had only been a few minutes. She stood and put the photo on the blanket with the other one before going to the bathroom and blowing her nose with the cheap rough toilet paper her mother had to buy in order to save money. She looked at herself in the mirror and took a deep breath.

Time to keep moving, she thought. *If Mom ever taught me anything, it was how to be strong. Things may not be how I want them to be, but I have to believe that I have the power to make the most out of it.* Leaning over the sink she turned on the water and splashed water on her face.

I can do this. I can still go to college if I keep working hard. At least I won't have to go to the library to do my homework and study anymore. Maybe this is a blessing in disguise. I have to take the bad with the good because I really don't have any choice. Then she felt guilty for even thinking that her mother's murder could be a blessing in disguise.

Holly dried her face and began to go through the things in the bathroom. She pulled out a bottle of her mother's perfume and a couple of her favorite fingernail polishes. After adding them to the collection on the couch, she slowly walked down the hall to her mother's room.

She knew she wanted to take most of the things in her own room with her, so she didn't feel the need to sort through it first. No, for now she needed to do the hard stuff alone. It was really nothing new to her. She'd been alone and dealing with the hard stuff for so many years by herself, she didn't feel comfortable doing it in front of people who were virtually strangers.

It wasn't that Holly didn't like Brigid and Linc. She thought they were great people, and she trusted them completely. It was just that she didn't want others to know how vulnerable she was. She'd kept all of her problems inside for so long, it was going to take a lot of time before she would feel comfortable talking about them.

She opened her mother's bedroom door, feeling the heavy sadness return, but instead of trying to hide from it she allowed the feelings free rein. She smiled, laughed at some memories, and cried at others. She picked out a few trinkets her mother had loved and even a few items of clothing.

By the time she was finished, the pile on the couch was quite large. Each item represented a memory or a part of her life that she wasn't ready to let go of quite yet. When she placed the last item on the couch, she felt she was ready for whatever the future brought. Holly went to the front door and opened it, waving for Linc and Brigid to come in.

Linc closed the door behind them. Brigid took one look at Holly's face and said, "Oh, honey." She pulled the young girl into her arms. At first, Holly stiffened, but the longer Brigid held her the more relaxed she became, until she felt safe enough to cry.

Her body shook with deep racking sobs, her face buried in Brigid's shoulder. Brigid turned her head and softly kissed Holly's hair, her own tears starting to fall. Linc walked over to them and wrapped his arms around them, pulling them in close to him. They stayed that way until Holly stopped crying, all of them feeling unbelievably close to each other in that long poignant moment.

CHAPTER FIFTEEN

"Are you sure this is all you want?" Brigid asked after they'd loaded the last bag into the back of Linc's truck.

Holly stood in the middle of the kitchen and looked around. Her eyes landed on the small notebook that had been pushed to the side, the note her mother had left her last night still facing the ceiling. Holly picked up the notebook and flipped the cover closed. She slipped it in her pocket before she turned toward Brigid and Linc. "Yeah, I think so." Holly smiled slightly. "Most of it's just stuff, you know?"

"If you change your mind, let me know. We can come back later or tomorrow if you think of anything else you want."

"Thanks, I will," Holly said.

"I don't know about you ladies, but I'm starving. I'm in the mood for some good, old fashioned, home cooking. How about coming over to my house for dinner tonight?" Linc asked as they climbed in the truck.

Brigid turned and looked at Holly. "That sounds great to me. What do you think, Holly? Want to try out Linc's cooking? He's pretty good."

"Sure, that would be fine," Holly said.

"Good," Linc said. "Does anything sound good? What's your favorite type of food?"

"Pasta, hands down." Holly said. "If I could have it every day, I would."

"Then I guess it's good that I was planning on making baked penne pasta with a carbonara sauce. I'm part Italian, so I cook a lot of pasta," Linc said. "How about if you two come over say, around 6:00? That will give us time to get these things back to your place. While you're getting settled, I'll go to the store to get what I need, and I'll have plenty of time to get it started."

"That sounds great," Brigid said. She was really glad that Linc and Holly were getting along so well. She liked having Holly around. It was odd having someone else in the house, but at the same time it was also a good feeling.

After the short drive across town to Brigid's they unpacked Linc's truck. When he left Linc promised he'd pick something up for dessert. As he pulled out of the driveway, he leaned out his window and said, "I'm assuming anything with chocolate would be fine with both of you, would I be right?"

"That you would be," Brigid said with a laugh.

"He really likes you," Holly said as they lugged the last bag into her room.

"You think?" Brigid asked.
"Oh, yeah. Definitely," Holly said with a knowing smile.

"What makes you say that?" Brigid asked as she started pulling clothes out of one of the bags and folding them.

"It's just the way he looks at you when you aren't paying attention. And when you talk? He gets this sparkle in his eyes. Have you two been together for a while?" Holly asked as she started taking items out of another bag and arranging them on the shelves in the closet.

"We've been seeing each other for a few months now. We're not trying to make a big deal out of it," Brigid said. "Just kind of seeing where it takes us."

Holly stopped and looked at Brigid, "Have you met his parents?"

Brigid paused before saying, "Yes."

"Oh, then he's definitely serious," Holly said as she returned to putting her things away.

"What makes you say that, and how do you know all of this?" Brigid asked incredulously.

"I read a lot. Sometimes when I got bored I'd read some of the self-help books at the library. A lot of them are on relationships and stuff like that, so I have a pretty good sense about when a relationship is getting serious," Holly said with a smirk.

Brigid laughed. "You're kind of a crazy kid, you know that?"

Holly shrugged. "Well, you just never know when something you read will become important to you. I love reading books, and it was kind of interesting to read about different human behaviors and then watch them in action."

They continued to go through the things Holly had brought to the house and organize them. Brigid decided Holly needed a new desk and another set of shelves. After arguing with Holly about whether or not they were needed, she went online and ordered them. When she was finished Holly thanked her and agreed they'd look great in her room, even though she'd told Brigid she was perfectly happy with the furniture that was already in there. Brigid told her it was a done deal and that the furniture would be delivered in two weeks.

When they were finished they got Jett and headed over to Linc's house. It had been a long and emotional day for both of them, so it felt good to get outside for a while. Jett was between them, because he was having a difficult time deciding which one of them he wanted to be next to on the short walk to Linc's house. Once they were past the treeline and he saw Linc's house, they were both forgotten. He ran as fast as his legs would take him. Holly and Brigid looked at each other and laughed, but then Holly became concerned and said, "Do you want me to chase him?"

"No, this is why I didn't put a leash on him. I knew my arm would have been pulled off as soon as he saw Linc's house. He knows where we're going now, and trust me, he'll be there well before us." She laughed as she watched from a distance and saw Jett jump on Linc's front door, scratching to get in. A moment later they saw Linc open the door only to be greeted by a huge hairy black dog.

Linc greeted the excited dog and said, "Hey, Jett. Did you bring me some company?" A few moments later when Brigid and Holly arrived Linc gave Brigid a kiss and followed the two of them into the house. As Brigid had told Holly, Linc was an excellent cook and they thoroughly enjoyed his dinner, to say nothing of the chocolate brownies topped with chocolate ice cream.

*****

The next morning Brigid and Holly went to her school to talk with Principal Bartlett.

"Good morning, Holly. I'm so sorry to hear about your mother," he said softly. "If there's anything I can do…" He let it trail off as he led them into his office. He shut the door, turned to Brigid, and said, "You must be Brigid."

"Yes, I am," she said shaking his hand. "It's nice to meet you."

"Please, have a seat," he said gesturing towards the two chairs opposite his desk. The principal's office looked much like any other school office. The walls were painted an off-white and there were motivational posters on every wall. "I think the first thing we should talk about is what the school and I can do to help you, Holly," he said as he steepled his fingers under his chin and looked at her. "Your teachers and I want you to continue the excellent path you're on with your education, but we also realize you probably need a little time to process everything that has happened."

He turned to Brigid and said, "Would you agree with that?"

"I certainly would," Brigid said as she nodded approvingly. "But it doesn't matter what I think. I want to leave any decision regarding school up to Holly. I think she's old enough to decide for herself what she wants to do."

"Absolutely," Principal Bartlett said. "How would you like to handle things, Holly? We've only got about six weeks of school left until the end of the school year. It's really not that long."

Holly began to chew on the inside of her cheek as she tried to decide what she wanted to do. "It's not that I don't think I could do the work. It's just that I'm worried about, you know..." she motioned to the hallway that was nearby.

"The other students," Principal Bartlett said, finishing the sentence for her.

Holly nodded. "When we walked in, I saw how some of them looked at me. I think it would be hard for me to focus on my studies if I came back to school now."

Brigid had also noticed how the other students had stared at Holly when they walked into the school, and she couldn't blame them. They were just curious. She was sure all of the students had heard what happened, and even though they were concerned, for a girl like Holly, who was used to staying in the background and not attracting attention to herself, it was unsettling.

"Well, let's try this," Principal Bartlett said. "You can continue your studies from home, independently, until you feel ready to come back. If that doesn't happen before the end of the school year, that's completely fine. I know you're capable of doing the work. I've spoken to all of your teachers and they agree. Here's the work for this week." He tapped his fingertips on the top of a manila envelope and a couple books which were on the side of his desk. "I'm sure you already have their email addresses in case you have any questions, but I've also put them in the envelope."

"Thank you very much, Mr. Bartlett," Holly said, visibly brightening. She loved doing schoolwork, and she knew it was something that would take her mind off of everything that had happened. She didn't want to give up attending school but being around her fellow students right now was more than she could handle.

"Good, then that's settled." The principal slid the envelope and the books across the desk to Holly and smiled. "I mean it, Holly. Take all the time you need, and don't hesitate to reach out if you need anything. That goes for both of you." He smiled at Brigid. "Holly has impressed many of the faculty members with her hard work and dedication to her education. We all want nothing more than to see her succeed."

"I feel the same way, which is why I was willing to let her stay with me. I think she's got a very bright future ahead of her." Brigid patted Holly on her arm and smiled at her. She could tell Holly was feeling a bit nervous about all the praise and attention she was receiving.

"I think that just about wraps things up here," he said. "Brigid, if you could take a moment to update Holly's contact information with the school secretary, I'd appreciate it. You ladies have a wonderful day." Principal Bartlett escorted them out of his office and shut the door.

After stopping by the secretary's desk, they stepped into the hallway just as the bell was ringing. "Brigid, I need to stop by my locker and grab a few things," Holly said. "There are some folders and books in there I'm going to need for my homework."

"Lead the way," Brigid said. She followed Holly down the hall until she stopped at one of the lockers and started turning the dial.

"Holly? Is that you?" a male voice asked from behind them.

They turned and saw Wade standing in the middle of the hallway, a look of concern on his face. "I'm so glad to see you! How are you doing? How have you been?" The boy pulled Holly into his arms and held her for a moment. Brigid could see she was plainly surprised by the act.

"I'm okay," Holly said softly. "I'm still kind of trying to deal with everything."

"I'm sure it will take some time," he said. "I've been worried about you."

"Why don't you come by sometime?" Brigid offered. She didn't want to interrupt them, but she wanted to encourage Holly to invite her friends over. If she was going to be living at Brigid's home, she might as well be comfortable there.

"Are you sure?" Holly's eyes flashed with a look of surprise. It was as if she'd never even thought it was an option.

"Of course," Brigid said. "You can invite your friends over anytime. It will be good for you to have a friendly face come visit once in a while. Especially now that you're going to be doing your school work from home for a while."

"I was wondering how you were going to keep up those perfect grades." Wade smiled at them. "I'll talk to my parents. Could I have your telephone number?" He asked as he pulled out his phone.

Brigid gave him the house phone number and told him to feel free to call.

He turned back to Holly. "I'll call you tonight, okay? I gotta' go, or I'll be late to class. I'm so glad I saw you." He waved as he jogged off into the sea of students that were flooding the halls.

"Okay, that should be good," Holly said shutting her locker. They started walking toward the exit as the halls began to clear. "Thanks," she said.

"For what?" Brigid asked.

"For inviting Wade over," she said. "For giving him your number. I could have never done that before." She pushed open the metal and glass door that led out towards the front lawn of the school.

"Why not? Didn't your mom let you have friends over?" Brigid asked. She couldn't imagine Maggie not letting her daughter have slumber parties and sleepovers.

"No, I could have," she said as they walked down the sidewalk towards Brigid's car which was parked in the nearby parking area. "It's just that my mom wasn't always dependable. She'd forget to buy food or even come home some weekends. It was embarrassing. And if she was around, there was no telling what sort of state she would be in. I couldn't ask anyone to come over and witness that."

"Well you can now," Brigid said as they reached her car. "I remembered seeing you two at the library together, and I assumed you were friends."

"Kind of," Holly said as she buckled her seatbelt. "It's hard to explain."

Brigid started the car. "Let me guess, you like him."

Holly shrugged. "Maybe."

"Well don't worry, I won't embarrass you," she said with a laugh. "I remember being your age and how embarrassing my parents were. I promise I'll do my best not to be like that."

"Thanks, Brigid. I don't think you could be embarrassing if you tried." Holly said. "And believe me after what I've dealt with, you should be fairly easy to be around."

"I just want us to be able to get along. As long as we can manage that, I don't see us having any problems at all," Brigid said as she looked over at the young girl and smiled.

"I promise, I won't be any trouble to you. I'll do my best to always follow the rules. I don't want you getting mad at me and sending me away." This was something that had been weighing heavily on Holly's mind. She'd been concerned that Brigid would change her mind about letting her stay there.

"I'm not going to send you away, Holly," Brigid said softly. "I don't see you suddenly being a terrible kid. Sure, we're going to have our disagreements. I realize that will happen, but as long as we try to stay open and communicate, no matter what, I don't think things could ever get to that point." She glanced toward Holly, "You're safe now, Holly. Everything's going to be okay."

Holly sighed. "I'm trying. It's just after all these years…"

"I know, honey, I know," Brigid said as they drove home.

CHAPTER SIXTEEN

Brigid decided to drop Holly off at the house and then see if she could talk to Mark and MaryAnn Thompson. She left Holly and Jett curled up on the couch with the TV going and headed out in the hopes that she could narrow down the list of suspects. She didn't want to believe that her old classmates had been capable of murder, either one of them, but she knew she'd feel better if she could cross both of them off the list.

As she was driving across town to the furniture store the Thompsons owned, Brigid thought about the dinner the previous night with Linc and Holly. It was such a relief when they both started laughing and teasing each other. They were getting along so well by the end of the evening Brigid had to remind herself that she'd just introduced them to each other. It made Brigid much more confident that the arrangement with Holly was going to work out.

There were a few times Brigid caught herself feeling as though she must be crazy for taking on the care of a teenage girl whose mother had just been murdered. After all, what did she know about being a mother? Very little, but she was finding this child pseudo-mother thing made her feel good. For the first time in her life, she began to wonder what life would have been like if she'd had children. It wasn't that she wanted any of her own at this point. She was happy with the way things were going, but maybe it would turn out that Holly was the child she was supposed to have had.

She pulled into a parking space in front of Thompson's Furniture, determined to help find out who Maggie's killer was. She remembered the relief she'd felt when she'd put together who her friend Lucy's killer had been, and she wanted to give Holly the same satisfaction. Brigid had noticed the way Holly would look over her shoulder and look out the windows when she thought Brigid wasn't looking. She'd also heard the soft cries coming from behind Holly's bedroom door the night before. Brigid hoped that with the killer caught, Holly could begin to heal.

Brigid picked up her purse and climbed out of her car. She looked up at the old brick building and smiled as she remembered riding her bike to the store for a piece of candy after school. That was when Mark's grandfather was still alive and running the store with his father. He always had a piece of candy for any child who came in to visit him. He was a kind and gracious man, which was why Brigid hoped Mark had a good alibi. She didn't want to think of him as being the murderer.

As she pushed open the glass door, the little bell above it tinkled, signaling a customer had entered the store. She looked around the showroom but didn't see anyone. Brigid knew Mark would be out shortly, so she roamed through the rows of furniture. She wasn't exactly shopping, but she didn't mind looking either.

"Brigid, is that you?" a familiar male voice said.

"Mark, how are you doing?" Brigid asked as he came around a counter at the back of the store.

"Great, actually. We just got our new website up and running. Now we can accept payments online," he said, beaming.

"I'm sure that will be good for business," Brigid said as she ran her hand along the top of the nearest couch.

"I sure hope it will be. What can I do for you?" It was a smooth transition into salesman mode.

"I'm really just looking at the moment," Brigid sighed. "You may have heard I have someone living with me now..." she let the sentence trail off, watching Mark's reaction.

"Yes, I did," he said. "How's she holding up?" His concern was evident from his furrowed brow.

"As well as can be expected," she said.

Mark nodded. "Completely understandable. I was shocked when I heard about it. MaryAnn and I went into Denver on a date that night. We went to dinner and then out dancing at a new place that just opened up. It's called the Denver Dance Palace. It was just what we needed."

He looked toward the back room and then quietly whispered, "MaryAnn and I haven't been doing very well lately. We went in hopes of rekindling some of the romance and ended up staying until the place closed at one. It was a wonderful evening," he said, smiling.

"That's great!" Brigid said. "I'm so glad. I know how tough it can be once the spark has gone. I have a divorce under my belt to prove it."

Mark nodded solemnly. "It's true, it takes work. Hey, aren't you seeing that Linc guy?" he asked. "You two really should go to that new place. I bet I still have the receipt from our drinks." Mark began to pull pieces of paper out of his pocket, finally handing one to Brigid. "We got there around 10:00 that night, and there were already quite a few people there. Guess they're pretty concerned with security, because there were cameras and security guards everywhere."

Brigid took the receipt from him and looked at it. Mark was right. According to the time imprinted on the receipt, the bar bill had been paid by Mark with a credit card at 1:00 a.m. They'd been there until well after midnight, making it impossible for the two of them to have been back in Cottonwood Springs around midnight, the time when the coroner had concluded that Maggie had died.

"Do you mind if I hold onto this?" Brigid asked. She tried to make it appear as though she was interested in going to the Denver Dance Palace.

"Sure, I don't need it anymore." He looked around the showroom. "Say, would you happen to have a good bed for Maggie's daughter?" He waved Brigid over toward the far corner of the showroom where the beds were displayed.

"I have one that was already in the guest bedroom. To be honest, I'm not sure if it's any good or not." Brigid chuckled.

Mark looked back towards the counter and the door that led to the back offices. "I feel terrible that poor girl is an orphan. Especially just as her mother was getting clean. I really liked, I mean…" Mark caught himself about to admit something he wasn't sure Brigid knew.

"It's okay, Mark. I know." She looked toward the back of the store. "I won't be passing the information on. Maggie had a good heart, even if she didn't always do the right thing," she said diplomatically.

"I really did care for her, Brigid. I was even ready to leave MaryAnn for her, because things were so bad between us. I honestly didn't think we could ever again be happy together. When I was with Maggie, I felt like someone was really listening to me and understood me. It took a little soul-searching for me to realize MaryAnn has always had my heart, even when sometimes I didn't know it." Mark smiled at her.

"That's so sweet, Mark," Brigid said. "I'm happy for you. Believe me, I know marriage isn't always easy."

"No, it's not," he said, rubbing the back of his neck, "but it's worth it. Anyway, I'd like to help you out. If you need anything for her, just let me know, and I'll give you an excellent deal. You won't get a better price anywhere else. I don't care what it is. Before you buy anything, see me first."

"Thank you, Mark," Brigid said, touched by his generosity. "I'll remember that. I'll talk to her tonight about the bed and everything else. I might be back to take you up on your offer." She heard a sound coming from her phone, letting her know she had a text message. "I better go, but I'll let you know," Brigid said as she walked toward the front door.

"You do that. Good luck, Brigid. Stay safe." Mark raised his hand in a wave as Brigid slipped out the door. She pulled her phone out of her purse and saw a message from her sister.

Can you swing by the bookstore?

Brigid typed her response as she stood outside her car.

Sure. I'm just down the road. What do you need?

Brigid climbed into her car and was pulling on her seatbelt as the response came through.

Just get down here, geeze.

Brigid laughed. She could sense her sister's exasperation as she typed the text. She looked back at the furniture store and mentally crossed Mark and MaryAnn Thompson off the suspect list. If they went out to eat and then dancing, there was no way they would have made it back from Denver in time to murder Maggie. Especially since there were security cameras there.

If it came down to it, Brigid was sure there would be footage that showed them in Denver at the time Maggie had been murdered. Brigid sighed with relief. She really didn't want the murderer to be one of her classmates.

Brigid backed her car out from the parking spot in front of the furniture store. "I'll go see what the heck Fiona wants before I try to find out where Frank Sterling was at the time of the murder," she said to herself. She turned up the music on the car radio and sang along as she drove through the quiet streets of Cottonwood Springs.

There wasn't much traffic, so it didn't take long before she pulled up in front of her sister's bookstore.

Brigid recognized Missy's car and wondered what her sister was up to this time. When she approached the store, she saw Fiona and Missy seated in two of store's collection of mismatched armchairs, sipping coffee and talking. She pushed the door open, and they turned towards her.

"Hi, Brigid," they said in unison.

"You weren't busy, were you?" Missy asked.

"Brigid's never busy," Fiona teased. "I'm starting to think all she does is drive around all day."

"Cute, Fiona, cute," Brigid said, smiling. She knew her sister loved to tease her. "What's up, ladies?"

"Come sit," Missy said, patting the chair next to her. "Join us in a cup of coffee."

Brigid poured herself a cup and sat down.

"Apparently, news of your good deed has spread," Fiona said as she sipped her coffee.

"Oh?" Brigid asked. "What good deed would that be?"

"Fiona is just being a pain," Missy chided. "There are lots of people around town who have donated money and things to help Holly. I was just telling Fiona that I needed to get in touch with you and see what you want to do with all the stuff that has been donated."

"You're kidding," Brigid said, completely taken aback.

"Don't forget how much our town can come together," Fiona said. "We tend to take care of our own. Remember how long Henri got casseroles after Lucy's murder?"

"I remember," said Brigid. "I ended up with one of them, because he didn't think he could eat another tater tot casserole." She laughed. "So what kind of things are we talking about?"

"It's probably best if you come down to the church yourself when you get a chance. We have a corner in the basement where we're storing all of it for now. You should be happy not too many people know where you live, or they would have been showing up at your front door instead of the church." Missy smiled. "I spread the word that if anyone wants to help you out to bring it by the church first. That way you and Holly won't get too overwhelmed."

"That's amazing, Missy. Thank you so much." Brigid was quiet for a few moments as she thought about her schedule. "I can probably stop by the church later. I'll get Holly and bring her with me. That will give her a chance to decide what she wants and what she doesn't. Anything that we don't take you can give to someone else who's in need, can't you?"

Missy nodded. "Of course. There are always families in need around Cottonwood Springs and the neighboring communities. Believe me, that won't be a problem."

"Good," Brigid said sipping her coffee. "I took Holly to her school this morning. She's going to be doing her classwork at home for now."

"How are things going with her, anyway? I'm sorry I haven't been over yet to introduce myself. You know how it is here. I'm always busy," Fiona apologized.

"Don't worry about it, Fiona. Maybe I can bring her by later. She loves books, and she'd probably like to pick up a few here. She's spent a ton of time at the library. I think she's read every good book they have there."

"Sure, that would be great. I'd love to meet her. Missy says she's a great kid."

"She is," Brigid said. "I'm a little nervous about trying to take care of her, but I'm finding it's not as hard as I thought it might be."

"I don't think she'll give you any trouble," Missy said. "I remember when she came to the church's bible school for preschool children. At the time, Maggie just brought her to it so she wouldn't have to watch her for a few hours. She was a smart little girl even then."

"She's definitely smart, and she and Linc get along great, too."

"That's always good," said Fiona.

Brigid stood. "Well, I really need to get going. I have another stop to make before I can pick Holly up, come back here, and then go to the church. Plus, Sheriff Davis is supposed to be giving me a call."

"What for?" asked Fiona.

"He asked me to help him out with the investigation into Maggie's murder, like I did with Lucy's. I've been checking up on some suspects. They're having a hard time finding one of them. They're pretty sure he's at home, but he won't answer the door. Sheriff Davis is hoping if we show up together, with him in plain clothes instead of a uniform, maybe he'll answer the door."

"Probably worth a shot," Fiona said. "Make sure you get back to see me. You know I'm trapped here until closing time."

"Promise," Brigid said.

CHAPTER SEVENTEEN

Brigid left the bookstore and pointed her car in the direction of Frank Sterling's house. She'd gotten directions from Missy, who not only seemed to know everyone in town but also where they lived. As Brigid was driving towards his home, she wondered if Sheriff Davis' deputies had had any luck yet with Maggie's ex-boyfriend Billy or his and Maggie's mutual friend, Sam.

She pulled up in front of the Sterling house and parked on the street, sending a quick text to Sheriff Davis to find out if they'd made any headway. She put her phone in her purse, climbed out of her car, and walked up to the door.

Brigid had met Frank and his wife, Eve, a few times. They were on friendly terms, since it was a small town, and Eve had come to one or two of the book club meetings, but usually she was too busy and had to miss it. Brigid decided to use the book club as an excuse for why she'd come to visit.

As she knocked on the door, Brigid turned and looked at the Sterling's lawn and porch. The yard was freshly mowed, but the flower bed was overgrown with weeds. The cushions on the porch swing looked dirty and sad, as though nobody had sat there for a while. The leaves of the potted fern in the corner looked like it desperately needed a drink of water.

Brigid turned when she heard the door opening. "Yes?" It was Eve.

"I'm not disturbing you, am I?" Brigid asked.

"No, not at all, Brigid. Come in." Eve opened the screen door and stepped aside for Brigid to enter. The house was dark, with all the curtains and blinds drawn. It smelled musty and Brigid could see dust motes floating through the air where beams of the sunlight were slipping through the pulled drapes. The house was neat, but there was a heaviness in the air that was almost tangible.

"I'm sorry to just drop by, Eve. Missy told me where you lived. I wanted to ask you about the book we've been reading for this month's book club.

"Okay," Eve said, patting her short curly hair. "I've actually been able to read it this month," she said smiling. "Although it's probably terrible that I'm happy about that." She motioned for Brigid to sit on the couch. "Would you like anything to drink?"

"No, thank you," Brigid said. "Why would that be terrible?"

"I only got to read the book because Frank's father, Paul, has been in the hospital. He had a setback of sorts on Friday, and he's been there ever since. Frank and I spent all night Friday in the hospital with him. That's when I read the book. It was touch and go for a few hours with Paul," she said with a sigh. "I feel terrible for being relieved that someone else is able to care for him for a while, but it's been exhausting. I hate to admit it, but it's been nice to be able to rest and relax for a while."

"I can't say that I blame you. I'd think caring for someone in ill health the way you two do would be extremely taxing, not only on you, but on your marriage as well." Brigid knew she'd already found out what she came for, but she felt Eve could use the company, so she continued to talk to her.

"You'd think so, but so far I think Frank and I have gotten

stronger because of it. Granted, we hardly ever see each other. Yet, somehow, we've survived. I can't explain it." Eve smiled, but her eyes told Brigid she was tired.

"I'm glad. Do you think you'll be able to make it to the next book club meeting?"

"I can't make any promises yet, but I'll do my best," Eve said.

They talked for a little while longer and Brigid felt the conversation had given her a chance to get to know Eve better. Eve asked about Holly and how things were going with her, and Brigid filled her in.

"Well, I better get going, I still have a few errands to run today. Eve, let me know if you ever need anything. Honest, it's not a problem, even if it's just to chat," Brigid said as she stood up.

"I will, thanks." Eve stood up and followed Brigid to the door, too tired to realize that they never discussed why Brigid had come to visit in the first place.

As she walked to her car, Brigid's cell phone started to ring. She looked at the screen and saw it was Sheriff Davis.

"I've been meaning to call you," Brigid said as she answered.

"Good. Reckon that means you got somethin' fer me."

"I believe so," she said as she climbed in her car. "It looks like Mark and MaryAnn Thompson were in Denver the night of Maggie's murder. I have a receipt showing they were at a dance club late into the night, well past the suspected time of the murder."

Brigid heard scratching on the other end before Davis said, "Okay. If we need to down the line, we'll verify that with security cameras or whatever. I jes' took 'em off the list. That all?"

"I stopped by Frank Sterling's house and spoke to his wife, Eve.

She said his father, Paul, was admitted to the hospital on Friday. They were both there with him all night." Brigid continued.

"Okay. I'll make sure that's true by talkin' to whoever was on duty at the hospital that night. They'll be able to confirm they were there at the time of the murder. Good work," he said. "Wish my deputies were as successful as you are. Looks like I'm gonna' need ya' to help me out this afternoon after all." She heard the disappointment in his voice.

"I'm sure we'll make headway, don't worry about it," Brigid said.

"Hope yer' right. I don't see how both Samantha and Billy have been able to evade me and my men, but I can't force 'em to open their doors, leastways not without some sorta' proof."

"We'll worry about that when we get there," Brigid told him. "No sense in stressing over something that hasn't happened yet. You just call me when you're ready to head over there."

"Will do. I'm tellin' ya', Brigid, now I understand why my predecessor popped antacid chews like candy. This stuff can get stressful. I'll get a hold of ya' later," he said.

Brigid pulled away from the curb and headed towards home. When she got home, she talked to Holly and told her she had a few places she'd like to take her.

"So where are we going?" Holly asked as they buckled their seatbelts in Brigid's car

"First we're going to stop by the church. Apparently, people have been donating things to help you out. We're going to see what they have and then go to my sister's bookstore. She'd like to meet you, and I've been thinking about picking up a few books."

"Your sister owns the bookstore here in town? Read It Again?" Holly asked in a surprised tone of voice.

"Yes, why?" Brigid asked.

"Oh my gosh, I love that place. They have book club meetings and everything!" Holly was clearly excited.

"I go to those," Brigid said with a smile. "Don't tell me you're interested in sitting around with a bunch of older women talking about a book?"

"Definitely! That would be, like so awesome!" Holly said, practically bouncing in her seat.

"Okay, consider it done. You can come to the next one with me. Calm down," Brigid chuckled. She never imagined a teenager could get so excited over books. "Sometimes one of the members will suggest a book for the group, so maybe you can think about what you'd like to suggest when it's your turn. That way you'll be ready."

"I will," Holly said.

After they pulled up outside the church, they walked around to the side of the church and down some stairs that led to the basement. When they stepped inside, both of them stopped, shocked at the number of things that were there.

"Oh, my gosh," Holly said as she looked around. Missy was in the room, organizing all of the items that had been donated.

"Oh, good! I'm so glad you're here," Missy said as she turned around and greeted them. "Holly, please don't feel like you have to take everything that's here with you, and you don't need to go through it all right now either. You can come back as often as you need to. This room doesn't get used that much."

Brigid's eyes scanned over the collected items, in awe of what the community had done on its own. Missy was in the middle of organizing some clothing, taking things out of a large bag and folding them on a nearby table. There was a new mattress set, room decorations, more clothing, as well as a desktop computer, a big desk, and a few matching end tables.

"Holly, why don't you start going through the clothes I've folded over here? Some of this stuff looks like it would fit both of you, so when you're done, let Brigid take a look." Missy smiled as Holly began to carefully go through the things. "Brigid, may I speak with you for a moment?"

Missy pulled Brigid into the next room but left the door open. When she was sure Holly was distracted, she said, "The stuff in there is nothing compared to the money that's been donated. There's quite a bit. What do you want me to do with it?"

"I think I can support her, so I don't really need it." Brigid was quiet for a moment and then said, "Could you possibly put it in a college fund for her or some sort of a savings account?"

"That's a great idea!" Missy squealed. "I love it. I don't see why I couldn't. I'll open one up in her name, deposit it all there, and let it do its thing. When she's old enough, she can use it for whatever she wants, hopefully college. Great idea, Brigid."

Brigid smiled. "I think that would be the best use for the money everyone's donated. I can't believe so many people did this. It touches my heart."

"I know. Jordan only mentioned Maggie's death on Sunday in order to get everyone thinking about the way they treat others. He'd mentioned she had a daughter who would now grow up without her mother and so on. He never expected anyone to feel as though they had to give something to her. It started off with just one or two people donating things, but this morning we had a lot more." She sighed. "I love seeing our community coming together to do something like this, and totally by accident. It just goes to show that people are truly good."

"I agree," Brigid said. "We're going to have to leave soon, because I promised Holly I'd take her by the bookstore."

"I bet she'll love that," Missy said as they returned to the room containing the donations.

"Here's a pile of stuff I'd like," Holly said. "This other pile is of things that really aren't my style. I hope that doesn't sound ungrateful. It's not meant to be."

"No, that's fine, I'll set those things aside, and I'm sure someone else will be able to make use of them. If you give me a little time, I can get the things I haven't taken out of boxes and sacks organized for you, so it would be easier for you to sort through the next time you come. Would that be okay?" Missy asked Holly.

"Thank you, that would be great, but you don't need to do all that for me." Holly said. "I can manage."

"I insist," she said. "And if you want any of this furniture, I'm sure I can get someone to take it over to the house."

Holly looked at the new mattresses and the headboard in the corner. "Brigid already had a lot of this stuff in the bedroom when I moved in," she said.

"None of it has to stay, Holly," Brigid said. "I bought it all secondhand, just so there'd be something in the guest room. You won't hurt my feelings if you like this stuff better." She looked around and pulled one of the nightstand drawers open. "It really is a lot nicer and more modern than what's in your room now. I know what I'd choose if I were you."

"Brigid, are you sure you won't mind?" Holly asked.

"Not at all. We can donate what you don't want to someone else who needs it," Brigid said.

"I think I know just the people, too," Missy offered. "We can get it switched out in no time." She stood next to Holly and put her arm around her. "I want you to remember one thing about the people who donated these things. All of them care about you and want you to be happy, Holly. All of this was just for you."

Holly looked at Missy, tears starting to form in her eyes. "I won't. I can't believe it. It's crazy," she said.

"You deserve it," Missy said. "Now run along. Knowing Fiona, she's probably tapping her fingers waiting for you two down at the bookstore. Patience may be a virtue, but it's one Fiona doesn't possess. I'll get this sorted out in a day or so and I'll bet we'll have more things coming in."

Holly and Brigid thanked Missy again and headed back to her car. On the way to the bookstore, Brigid stopped at the gas station and picked up a candy bar for her sister. She knew Fiona would only take a bite or two of it, afraid of gaining even an ounce, but she knew she'd savor that bite.

"I brought you something," Brigid called out as the bell chimed over the door, signaling their entrance.

"Oh, goody. I was getting ready to make a snack," Fiona said as she came out from behind the counter. "Hello, you must be Holly," she said when she saw the young girl. She held out her hand, "It's nice to meet you."

Brigid did a short introduction before handing over the candy bar. "I know how much you love one," she said with a laugh.

"You bet I do," Fiona said tearing into it. She turned and looked at Holly, "Brigid tells me you're a reader, is that true?"

"Yes, ma'am. I love to read," Holly said politely.

"Please, call me Fiona," she said smiling. "Why don't you take a look around? Since you're living with my sister, I think that qualifies you for the family discount."

"A discount? Really?" she turned and looked at Brigid. "I have some money from tutoring, you won't mind, will you?"

"Not at all. Take your time," Brigid said. Holly clapped and did a little jump before disappearing between the rows of books.

"Cute kid," Fiona said savoring her bite of the candy bar. "She seems great."

"She is, and she's so helpful," said Brigid. "She's been doing chores around the house and in the yard without me even having to ask. She's even taken Jett for a walk."

"Good, I'm glad you've got company."

Their conversation was interrupted by Brigid's cell phone ringing. She looked at the screen and saw it was Sheriff Davis. She put the phone on speakerphone and answered, "Hi, Sheriff Davis. What's up?"

"Brigid, sorry this is short notice, but I jes' got a call from Billy's neighbor sayin' he and Sam were at Billy's place. Thought I could swing by and get ya' if you ain't too busy?"

"I'm at the bookstore with my sister and Holly," Brigid said.

"Go, she can stay here," Fiona mouthed to Brigid when she overheard what the sheriff said.

"You sure?" Brigid whispered. Fiona nodded.

"Corey, if you could pick me up at the bookstore, that would be great," Brigid said. "See you in a few minutes."

CHAPTER EIGHTEEN

"Really appreciate yer' help with this," Sheriff Davis said as he drove the unmarked police car he and Brigid were in towards Billy's house. "Know it ain't exactly an easy thing to do, tryin' to corner an addict."

"I don't mind," Brigid said as she watched the houses pass by. "We need to find out who killed Maggie, for Holly's sake, if nothing else. If this helps us get answers, I'm all for it."

"If this don't work, I'm gonna' have to get more creative," he said.

"Something tells me we're going to get somewhere with this," Brigid said. "I don't know why."

"Hope yer' right, 'cuz we're here," the sheriff said. Brigid looked at the tired-looking apartment building where Billy lived and felt sad for him. She knew this guy was bad news, but she couldn't help but feel as though there were some people who were just dealt a bad hand to begin with. At some point, life's circumstances caused them to turn down the wrong path. She wondered if someone had taken the time to reach out to help Billy, maybe he wouldn't be in the place he now found himself.

Brigid followed Corey up the short stairs to the front door. The screen door was ripped and flapping in the breeze. Corey lifted his hand and knocked on the side of the door.

Brigid turned towards Corey, certain she heard movement inside. The look on his face said he'd heard it, too. When no one answered, he knocked again. This time he opened the screen door and rapped directly on the door. In a few moments, a woman answered the door.

"Can I help you?" she asked as she barely pulled the door open and wedged her body into the narrow crack.

"Howdy, ma'am. We're just lookin' for Billy Watkins. Would he happen to be around?"

The woman bit her lip as she ran her fingers through her short curly blonde hair. "I'm afraid you just missed him."

"Know where he went?" Corey asked.

"He just went to the store." Her eyes darted around outside, as if she was looking for something or someone.

"I see," Corey said. "We're with the county. Mind if I ask a few questions?"

The woman looked from Corey to Brigid and back again. "I don't see what harm there could be in answering a few questions," she responded while remaining securely wedged in the slightly opened door.

Corey lifted his collar. "Mind if we step inside? It's gettin' a bit warm out here."

Brigid watched as the woman looked around inside and realized she couldn't come up with a reason to say no. "Sure, come on in."

Brigid stepped into the small apartment which smelled of stale cigarette smoke and body odor. The smell was so overwhelming she had to consciously keep herself from showing her revulsion.

"Thank you kindly, ma'am," Corey said as the woman shut the door behind them. If he smelled the horrible stench, his face didn't show it.

"Not a problem. What do you want to know?" she asked, looking down the hallway nervously.

Corey pulled out a small notebook and a pen. "First, I need your name. Just fer the record."

Brigid noticed that Corey wasn't exactly lying. He was in fact with the county, and he did have some questions to ask. She was impressed by his ability to think on his feet.

"Sam Rogers," she said rubbing her arm. "Now I don't want my name going on anything..." she started to say.

"Oh, don't worry. So, tell me Sam, do ya' live here?"
"No, my boy... I mean this is my friend's house."

Brigid and Corey exchanged glances before he said, "Ya' said he went to the store?"

"Sure did, I don't know when he'll be back," she said with a smile, her confidence returning.

"I see," Corey said. "Well, we're supposed to look around random homes to get a feel for what our local residents are strugglin' with when it comes to maintainin' their homes. Weatherization and all that. Ya' don't mind if I take a quick look-see, do ya'?" Corey began to walk toward the hallway.

"Well I don't think..." She faltered. Sam began to follow Corey down the hallway, but Brigid grabbed her arm and held her back. Sam turned and looked at Brigid.

"It will be brief. He won't take but a minute," Brigid said.

"Hey, wait, aren't you that lady who helped the sheriff when Lucy died?" Sam said in a startled voice. Brigid saw the realization set in as Sam's eyes widened, and she turned towards the direction Corey was headed as he walked down the hallway. "Billy, it's the sheriff! Run!" Sam screamed just as Corey was pushing on a door leading to the hallway that was partially cracked open.

As he opened the door, Corey saw Billy come flying out of a closet on the far side of the room and make a run for the wide-open window on the other side.

"Freeze!" Sheriff Davis yelled as he pulled out his gun which had been hidden by his jacket. Billy began pushing himself up to the window, having no intention of stopping.

Sam broke free from Brigid's grip and started running down the hall. "Leave him alone!" she screamed.

Brigid darted after her, easily catching up to her and holding her back before she could jump on Corey. He glanced back to see that Brigid had Sam restrained before holstering his weapon and grabbing Billy by the ankles just as he was about to make it out the window. In one solid jerk, he pulled Billy back into the room and threw him onto the floor. Corey pulled out a pair of handcuffs and snapped them on Billy.

"Recommend ya' stay put, boy," he said gruffly. He pulled out his cell phone and punched speed dial for the sheriff's office. "Sheryl, send three or four deputies over to the Watkins place," he barked into his phone. "Make it quick. Code three."

"Look, I didn't mean to," Billy started to yell. "It was an accident." He was talking so loudly Brigid was sure the neighbors could hear.

"Billy, ya' have the right to remain silent..." Corey said as he began to read him his Miranda rights. Once he was finished he looked at Brigid who was still holding on to Sam. "Don't let her go anywhere. Keep her right there."

Brigid nodded and held fast to the small woman, grateful she'd recently been working out at the gym. Otherwise, the fighting and flailing woman might have been a challenge. It wasn't long before the deputies Corey had summoned showed up and handcuffed Sam, reading the Miranda rights to her, as well.

"Seriously, Sheriff. I didn't mean to hurt her," Billy said as one of the deputies took Sam outside.

She could still be heard screaming. "Billy, don't tell them anything!"

"Who didn't ya' mean to hurt?" Sheriff Davis asked as he knelt down in front of Billy.

"Maggie. I didn't mean to hurt Maggie," Billy said. "I love her. It's just when I heard her talking about all the bad things she'd done, including what she'd done to me and the part about her leaving me and being better off without me, I just snapped."

"Whaddya' mean, ya' snapped?" Corey asked.

"I grabbed the nearest thing I could find and just wrapped it around her throat. I only wanted her to stop talking. I didn't want to hear those words come out of her mouth anymore. I just, I just, I didn't want to kill her, but I guess I did." He broke down in sobs and slammed his head against the floor.

"Relax, Billy." Corey patted him on the shoulder. "It's all over now, no more runnin'. So, where's the thing ya' wrapped around her neck?"

"It's… it's in a box in my bedroom," Billy said between sobs.

"Take him down to the station," Corey said to one of his deputies who had entered the room with his gun drawn as a backup for Sheriff Davis. "I'll be there in a coupla' minutes."

"How did you know what room he was in?" Brigid asked after Billy had been taken outside by the deputy.

"Jes' a feelin', I guess." As Corey crossed the hallway and entered a second bedroom, he slipped on a pair of rubber gloves. He found a trinket box on the nightstand next to the unmade bed. He carefully lifted the lid which revealed the missing tieback from the church. "Looks like we got us our murder weapon," he said.

Brigid stared at the small mundane piece of decorative rope which had been used to kill Maggie. "It's hard to believe something that little took her life," Brigid said.

"Hard drugs and alcohol took her life, this was just a tool," Corey said as he closed the lid on the box. "Bag this up," he said when one of his deputies walked in the room. "Need one of ya' to give Brigid here a ride back to her sister's bookstore," he said. Turning to Brigid he said, "Thanks fer bein' here. If I woulda' come by myself, Sam mighta' jumped me, and he'd have gotten away. Ya' saved my skin."

"It's the least I could do," Brigid said. "I'm just glad we know who did it."

"Agreed. By the way, how's Holly doin'?" Corey asked.

"Good," Brigid said. "She has her moments of sadness, but she's a strong young woman."

"That she is. Ya' don't even wanna' know what that kid's been through. I need to come see her. Maybe I'll have time now," he said looking around the room.

"She'd like that. We'll make you dinner if you stop by around supper time," Brigid said.

"I can take you to the bookstore, ma'am," one of the deputies said.

Brigid nodded and turned back to Corey. "Be safe," she said.

"Always," was his response.

On the drive back to the bookstore, Brigid felt a huge sense of relief wash over her. Now she could tell Holly that her mother's killer would be behind bars as well as the woman who was trying to help him cover up his crime. Sam was obviously trying to help Billy get away with it, probably for her own gain.

As she got out of the sheriff's car in front of the bookstore, Brigid noticed that Fiona and Holly were looking out the front window. Their eyes were wide, and their expressions showed they were shocked that Sheriff Davis hadn't brought her back. Instead, she'd arrived back at the bookstore in a black and white patrol car.

"What happened? We heard the sirens," Fiona said as soon as she walked in the door.

"They caught him," Brigid said, turning to Holly. "Billy did it. He killed Maggie."

The color drained from Holly's face. "Are you sure?" she asked.

Brigid nodded. "Yes, Sam was helping him hide out. Once he was caught, he confessed." She opened her arms and pulled the girl toward her. "It's over."

Holly wrapped her arms around Brigid before pulling back, tears running down her cheeks, but she was smiling. "Good. Mom deserved justice."

"I agree," Brigid said.

"While you were out playing Columbo, Holly and I came up with something we want to talk to you about," Fiona said.

Holly nodded. "Brigid, if you aren't okay with it, just say so, but I really hope you're fine with it," she said.

"Oh? What is it?"

"Well, you know I'm always here at the store, and I never really have time to take a decent break," Fiona began.

"Right, once you said something about hiring someone part time, but it never happened." Brigid walked over to the coffee pot and poured a cup. They all sat down in the armchairs in the open middle area of the store.

"Exactly. You know I'm fairly picky, though. I only wanted to hire someone who loved books as much as I do," Fiona said.

"Good luck with that," Brigid joked as she rolled her eyes and made a face. Holly laughed as the friendly banter between the sisters continued.

"Well thanks to you, dear sister, I have. I'd really like to have Holly come work for me, with your permission, of course." Fiona sat back in her chair, sipping her coffee.

Brigid turned to Holly. "Is this something you'd like to do? I mean my sister can be pretty pushy. Are you sure?" she asked.

Holly nodded emphatically. "Definitely! I love this place already. I was helping Fiona while we waited for you to come back."

"Holly helped me organize the back room," Fiona said.

"Oooh, that's a big undertaking," Brigid said raising her eyebrow.

"I'm well aware of it, but once I showed Holly the mess back there, she started organizing it and creating a locator system for the used books. She did a great job." Fiona smiled at Holly who looked like she'd just been awarded the Nobel Prize.

"I don't have any problem with it, as long as she gets paid fairly and still has plenty of time for her school work," Brigid said, wondering if she was saying the things a mother would say.

Holly jumped up and squealed. "I promise, Brigid, I won't let my grades slip one bit. Thank you so much." She leaned over and hugged

Brigid before turning to Fiona. "Do you mind if I go finish what I was doing?"

"Knock yourself out," Fiona said, motioning towards the back room. Holly skipped her way around the counter and to the rear of the store. "You'd think we just took her to meet the Backstreet Boys."

"I don't think they're popular anymore, Fiona, Anyway, you're the one who's always reading the latest magazines about the stars, so, who is popular now?" Brigid asked with a laugh.

"I skip over that stuff. Geeze." Fiona laughed. "Nothing like having a kid around to make you feel old."

"I'm quickly learning that to be a true statement," Brigid said.

"So, exactly when did you turn into a crime fighting superhero?" Fiona asked as she tucked her feet up under her.

"Well, it all started back when we were kids. I was stung by a radioactive bee," Brigid said with a laugh.

"You may think it's a joke, but you're going to get a reputation after this. You just wait and see," Fiona said wagging her finger at her older sister.

"I didn't do anything. I was just there helping Sheriff Davis," Brigid said as she held her hands up in mock surrender.

"I wonder how Linc's going to like you helping catch another bad guy. Have you told him yet?"

"No, I haven't," Brigid said as she pulled out her phone.

Fiona put her hand on Brigid's phone and pushed it down. "Go see him. It would be better if you told him in person. I'll bring Holly home in a few hours. You deserve some alone time," Fiona said with a knowing wink.

EPILOGUE

It didn't take long before word got out that Maggie Lewis' killer had been caught. Between the yelling Samantha had done and the neighbors seeing Samantha and Billy led out of his apartment in handcuffs, everyone in town pretty much knew by dinner time.

A week after Billy was caught, Holly returned to school. She was surprised by how kind and friendly the other kids were to her. Even Amanda kept her snide remarks to herself, although she still gave Holly dirty looks. That didn't bother Holly, though. Things were finally starting to work out for her.

Two days a week after school and on the weekends, Holly worked at the bookstore with Fiona. She loved every minute of it and had become the official person in Cottonwood Springs to ask for your next book recommendation, especially if you're looking for a suitable book for a teenager.

She helped Fiona build out the young adult section in the store and has recently started a book club for the younger crowd. She still makes time to help out her fellow students with tutoring during the school year. She's made a couple of new friends and has been hanging out with Wade a bit more often.

"This is really good, Brigid," Wade said, as they sat at the new dining room table Brigid had recently purchased from the

Thompson's furniture store. And yes, she'd gotten a very good deal on the purchase price.

"Thanks, Wade," Brigid said. "What do you think, Holly?"

"I hate to say it, but I think Linc still has you beat on this one," Holly said as she took another bite of her pasta.

Linc laughed and pounded his fist on the table, "I told you! I am the Pasta King!" He raised his hands in the air in celebration while everyone else laughed.

"Okay, Pasta King. Why don't you help me clean up the dishes?" Brigid said.

Linc stood up and started to take his empty plate to the kitchen area. "It would be my pleasure," he said as he slipped up behind Brigid and wrapped his free arm around her. He dotted kisses along her neck.

"Hey, there are young people in the room," Holly said, but she was smiling. She secretly enjoyed seeing Brigid and Linc together. She knew they were taking things slow and easy, but she couldn't help but hope they'd end up getting married.

"Are you going to go to the funeral with us tomorrow, Holly?" Brigid asked. Paul Sterling had passed away in his sleep just days after Billy was arrested. Frank and Eve had been at his bedside when it happened. Both of them were sad to see him go but relieved they no longer had to watch him twenty-four hours a day, seven days a week.

"I can't. I told Fiona I'd watch the store for her, so she could go," Holly said as she bit into a slice of garlic toast.

"Oh, that's right. She mentioned it, and I forgot," Brigid said.

"How do you like working there, Holly?" Linc asked.

"I love it!" Holly exclaimed. "Fiona's letting me pick out some new books whenever she places an order and we're going to be expanding the Young Adult section. She never realized just how good they were, and how many people would buy them," she said, smiling proudly.

"Good, I'm happy for you. It's always great to have a job you love. That way it doesn't feel like you're even working," Linc said as he scraped some scraps left over from dinner into Jett's dog dish. Jett ate them as fast as they touched the dish.

"Yep, and when school is officially out, we're starting a book club for teens. Fiona noticed that most of her customers were adults, so we're trying to change that," Holly boasted.

"Now that sounds like fun," said Brigid. "You kids can finish up in the front room, if you want. I know your favorite show will be coming on any minute."

Holly and Wade picked up their plates and darted off toward the couch, Jett hot on their heels.

"I'm so glad she's happy," said Brigid.

"Things really seem to be working out," Linc said. "Have you heard any more about Billy and Sam?"

Brigid looked toward the front room to make sure Holly and Wade weren't listening. "Corey told me they have Billy on suicide watch. After his hearing and finding out the extent of the charges against him, I guess he lost it. He keeps telling everyone he just wants to be with Maggie."

"That's too bad," said Linc. "But being unbalanced is no excuse for what he did."

"I agree," said Brigid. "And I guess Sam still thinks there's hope for the two of them. I heard she's been writing him every day from her cell. I'm fairly certain he hasn't replied."

"They don't allow inmates to write each other, do they?" Linc asked.

"I don't know if they're delivered to him, but she's been writing him. I just wish they could have charged her with more," Brigid sighed.

"Agreed. She may not have done it, but she knew Billy did and tried to help him get away with it." Linc shook his head. "What's wrong with people these days?"

"Have no idea," Brigid said, "but I feel better knowing there are two less bad guys out there."

"Speaking of bad guys, I hope you don't plan on making a habit of this crime fighting business," Linc said as he rinsed a plate.

"Oh no, not you too." Brigid leaned her head back and looked at the ceiling.

"I know, but hear me out. I don't want you making a name for yourself as being the person who catches the bad guys. Otherwise, the bad guys might start looking for you." He pointed the plate in his hand at her. "You need your own gun."

"No, I bought pepper spray. It's in my purse right now. Plus, I signed up for self-defense classes. I have to drive out of town for them, but I think it will be worth it."

"Good, I don't want anything happening to my special baby," Linc said as he kissed Brigid.

"Oh, speaking of baby… Did you hear about Mark and MaryAnn Thompson?" Brigid asked.

"No, what?"

"MaryAnn's pregnant!" Brigid said. "I guess they'd been trying forever and had finally given up. That was about the time their relationship started falling apart. Now, they're stronger than ever and she's expecting."

"That's a happy ending. Guess it's a good thing they took their furniture business online. I heard they've been doing even better now that their customers can shop on the internet," Linc said. "Although, I'd never buy a couch without sitting on it first."

Brigid laughed. "Agreed."

They finished loading the dishwasher just as there was a knock on the door.

"I'll get it," Brigid said. She hurried to the door and peeked outside to see who it was. She opened the door and said, "Sheriff Davis, what are you doing here?"

"Hey, Brigid, Linc. Jes' on my way home and thought I'd stop in and say 'hello'. How's Holly doin'?"

"Good, she's in the great room. Care to join us?"

"Sounds good," Corey said as he shut the door behind him.

"By the way, Corey," Linc said. "Brigid's helped you twice with investigations. Sure would be nice if she didn't have to do that anymore. Makes me worry about her."

"I can unnerstan' that, but in a town this small, can't believe we'll be havin' any more problems. I'm sure this was the last of 'em. Not to worry," he said as he walked into the great room.

Linc looked at Brigid and said, "I'd like to believe him, but I do think you have a talent for this and that's what worries me."

She put her arms around him and said, "Like the sheriff said, 'Not to worry.' Hopefully, Cottonwood Springs won't be seeing another murder for a long, long time."

RECIPES

CREAM CHEESE BROWNIES

Ingredients:
8 oz. pkg. cream cheese, room temperature
5 jumbo size eggs
½ tsp. vanilla extract (Don't use imitation!)
1 cup plus 5 tbsp. unsalted butter, room temperature, cut into 16 pieces
2 1/3 cups sugar
1 cup unsweetened cocoa powder
1 cup all-purpose flour
1 cup sugar (for the frosting)
5 tbsp. unsalted butter (for the frosting)
1/3 cup milk
6 oz. pkg. semi-sweet chocolate chips

Directions:
Preheat oven to 350 degrees. Coat a 9" x 13" baking dish with nonstick cooking spray.

Filling:
Put the cream cheese, 1/3 cup sugar, 1 egg, and vanilla into a food processor and process until smooth. Remove from processor and place in a bowl.

Batter:
Put the 16 pieces of butter, 2 cups sugar, and 4 eggs in a food processer and process until smooth. Add the cocoa and pulse 4 or 5 times. Add the flour and pulse until it is fully mixed.

Spread half the chocolate batter over the bottom of the prepared pan. Dot with the cream cheese filling, then top with the remaining half of the chocolate batter. Gently swirl the batter and filling with a rubber spatula. Bake until a skewer inserted into the center comes out with some crumbs on it, approximately 35 – 40 minutes. Let cool until just warm.

Frosting:
In a small saucepan combine 1 cup sugar, remaining 5 tbsp. butter and milk. Bring to a boil and continue boiling for one minute, stirring constantly. Remove from heat and stir in the chocolate chips until smooth. Pour over the warm brownies. Cool on a rack for 10 minutes and while still warm, cut into 24 2" squares. Enjoy!

LINC'S ITALIAN STYLE POT ROAST

Ingredients:
3 cloves garlic, minced
2 tsp. salt
1 tsp freshly ground pepper
2 tbsp. olive oil
4-pound eye of the round roast
1 cup onion, finely chopped
4 carrots, finely chopped
2 ribs celery, finely chopped
2 tsp. dried rosemary
1 cup red wine (Only use something you'd drink!)
2 15.75 oz. cans crushed plum tomatoes with juice
2 cups beef broth (I use the Better Than Bouillon concentrate.)

Directions:
Sprinkle the garlic, salt, and pepper over the roast, rubbing them

in. Heat the oil in a large Dutch oven over medium-high heat. Add the roast and brown on all sides.

Remove the roast from the pan and add the onion, carrot, celery, and rosemary. Cook, stirring, until the vegetables are softened, about 8 minutes. Transfer the vegetables to a slow cooker including any browned bits from the bottom of the pan. Stir in the wine and tomatoes. Add the roast and beef broth. Cook on high in the slow cooker 4 to 5 hours. When fork tender, reduce heat to low until ready to serve. Enjoy!

CRUSTLESS QUICHE LORRAINE

Ingredients:
8 jumbo size eggs
2 cups heavy cream
½ tsp. freshly ground black pepper
6 dashes Tabasco sauce
2 scallions, finely chopped
8 strips bacon, cooked until crisp, drained on a paper towel, and crumbled
3 cups finely shredded Swiss cheese

Directions:
Preheat oven to 350 degrees. Coat a 10" pie pan with nonstick cooking spray.

In a large bowl whisk together the eggs, cream, salt, pepper, and Tabasco. Stir in the scallions, bacon, and cheese, whisking until blended.

Pour the quiche batter into the prepared pan and bake until a knife inserted into the center comes out clean and the quiche has puffed up above the rim of the pie pan, 40 to 50 minutes. Set aside to cool. It will shrink as it cools, and that's okay.

Serve warm or at room temperature. Enjoy!

Baked Penne alla Carbonara

Ingredients:
1 cup unsalted butter
½ cup chopped shallots
1 tsp. fresh thyme
¼ cup all-purpose flour
1 ½ cups heavy cream
½ cup chicken broth
1 ½ cups Parmesan cheese (Please don't use the one that comes in a can.)
½ tsp. freshly ground pepper (or to taste)
Salt (to taste)
1 lb. penne pasta, cooked according to directions on package, and drained
2 tbsp. olive oil
12 strips bacon, cut into ½" pieces, cooked until crisp and drained on paper
towels
½ lb. fresh mozzarella cheese, cut into ½" cubes

Directions:
Preheat the oven to 350 degrees. Heat the butter in a saucepan over medium heat. Add the shallots and thyme. Cook, stirring, until softened, about 3 minutes. Whisk in the flour and cook, stirring constantly, until the flour is cooked but hasn't changed color, 3 to 4 minutes. Stir in the cream and chicken broth and bring to a boil, whisking constantly. Stir in 1 cup of Parmesan cheese and season to taste with salt and pepper.

Coat a 9" x 13" baking dish with nonstick cooking spray and sprinkle ¼ cup of the remaining Parmesan over the bottom. In a large bowl toss the cooked penne pasta with the olive oil.

Stir the sauce into the penne pasta, then stir in the bacon and mozzarella cheese. Transfer to the prepared pan and sprinkle the top with the remaining ¼ cup of Parmesan.

Bake the penne pasta until golden brown, about 30 minutes. Let rest for about 5 minutes before serving. Enjoy!

CARMELIZED BUTTERNUT SQUASH SOUP

Ingredients:
1 ½ tbsp. olive oil
1 large butternut squash, peeled down to the orange core and cut into small cubes
½ large onion, sliced
1 ½ tbsp. flour
½ tbsp. sea salt
½ tsp. white pepper
2 cups chicken broth
2 tbsp. honey
¼ cup heavy whipping cream
Pinch of ground nutmeg
Salt and pepper to taste

Directions:
Heat olive oil in a large pot over high heat. Stir squash in and brown, about 10 minutes. Stir onion, butter, sea salt, and white pepper into the squash. Cook until the onions are tender, about 10 minutes.

Pour chicken broth and honey over the mixture. Bring to a boil. Reduce heat to medium-low and simmer until the squash is tender, about 5 minutes

Pour the mixture into a food processor until half full. Cover and hold lid in place. Pulse a few times and then puree until smooth. (You may have to do this in batches.)

Return mixture to pot over medium heat. Stir in cream, and salt and pepper to taste. Serve and enjoy!

Paperbacks & Ebooks for FREE

Go to www.dianneharman.com/freepaperback.html and get your FREE copies of Dianne's books and favorite recipes immediately by signing up for her newsletter.

Once you've signed up for her newsletter you're eligible to win three paperbacks. One lucky winner is picked every week. Hurry before the offer ends!

ABOUT THE AUTHOR

Dianne lives in Huntington Beach, California, with her husband, Tom, a former California State Senator, and her boxer dog, Kelly. Her passions are cooking, reading, and dogs, so whenever she has a little free time, you can either find her in the kitchen, playing with Kelly in the back yard, or curled up with the latest book she's reading.

Her award winning books include:

Cedar Bay Cozy Mystery Series

Cedar Bay Cozy Mystery Series - Boxed Set

Liz Lucas Cozy Mystery Series

Liz Lucas Cozy Mystery Series - Boxed Set

High Desert Cozy Mystery Series

High Desert Cozy Mystery Series - Boxed Set

Northwest Cozy Mystery Series

Northwest Cozy Mystery Series - Boxed Set

Midwest Cozy Mystery Series

Midwest Cozy Mystery Series - Boxed Set

Jack Trout Cozy Mystery Series

Cottonwood Springs Cozy Mysteries

Coyote Series

Midlife Journey Series

Red Zero Series

Black Dot Series

Newsletter

If you would like to be notified of her latest releases please go to www.dianneharman.com and sign up for her newsletter.

Website: www.dianneharman.com,
Blog: www.dianneharman.com/blog
Email: dianne@dianneharman.com

PUBLISHING 11/23/18

WINE COUNTRY KILLER

BOOK FIFTEEN OF

THE CEDAR BAY COZY MYSTERY SERIES

http://getBook.at/WCK

Winery owners murdered in Sonoma, California. A serial killer on the loose. What's the connection? Will there be another murder?

A desperate call from a Sonoma County sheriff Kelly and Mike have helped before leads them to a winery guest house in Sonoma and then on to the Broadmoor Hotel in Colorado, searching for that connection.

Good thing they took their boxer dog, Rebel, with them. He's a master at preventing murders.

As always in this two-time USA Today Bestselling Author's cozy mysteries, there's plenty of food, mouth-watering recipes, and dogs.

Open your smartphone, point and shoot at the QR code below. You will be taken to Amazon where you can pre-order 'Wine Country Killer'.

(Download the QR code app onto your smartphone from the iTunes or Google Play store in order to read the QR code below.)

Made in United States
North Haven, CT
02 January 2023

30406347R00104